LOST TRADITIONS

THE CHRONICLES OF NEREZIA - 7

LOST TRADITIONS

Published by The Kraken Collective
krakencollectivebooks.com

Edited by Dove Cooper.
Cover by Eva I.
Character Portraits by Vanessa Isotton.
Interior Design by Claudie Arseneault.

claudiearseneault.com

ISBN: 978-1-0692516-7-1

The Chronicles of Nerezia

LOST TRADITIONS

THE CHRONICLES OF NEREZIA – 7

Claudie Arseneault

CINNIZE
SIOREZE
VIRZE
NEREZIA
(UPPER CONTINENT)

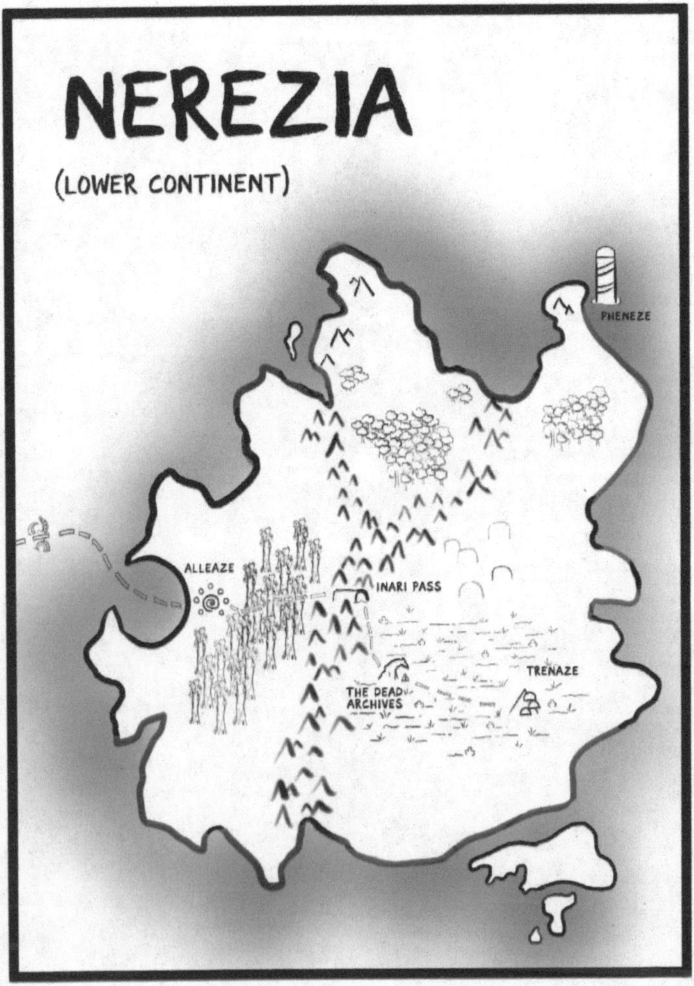

NEREZIA
(LOWER CONTINENT)
PHENEZE
ALLEAZE
INARI PASS
TRENAZE
THE DEAD
ARCHIVES

Horace (e/em), Embo Extraordinaire

Excitable and talkative, Horace has taken half-formed skills from eir many failed apprenticeships to become the Wagon's main cook.

Aliyah (she/her), Unwilling Hero

Left with the strange ability to transform into an eldritch tree and the memory of a mystical forest, the quiet and perceptive Aliyah is on a quest for answers.

Rumi (he/him), Anxious Artificer

Rumi travels the world in a magical Wagon and springs his marvelous creations on the isolated cities of Nerezia. He disguises protectiveness and anxiety under pessimism and grumpiness.

Keza Nesmit (she/her), Thorny Protector

Confident and abrasive, Keza is a thorny companion who knows her worth. Under the spikes hides fierce and loyal love.

The Wagon (it/it), Ancient Marvel

Once a legendary artificer, Rumi's Wagon of Wonderful Wares has gained increasing sentience as it travelled with Aliyah. Paternalistic and prideful at times, it is happy to serve as everyone's homes, so long as its genius is respected.

So far in
The Chronicles of Nerezia

Horace's trial day as a guard for eir home city of Trenaze should have been simple: stand watch, guide locals to the correct stalls, and guard the giant glyph that maintains one of the city's protective dome—the only thing that keeps away Fragments, shards that haunt the world and possess people.

But when a mysterious figure in a porcelain mask deactivates the dome, Fragments rush into the market, fusing into a monstrous amalgam. They are saved by a strange elf who can transform into a tree-like being, and who dissipated the Fragments with a single, eerie sentence: your story is my story.

When the elf collapses, Horace carries them to safety, to recover away from the panicked crowd and inevitable questions.

This stranger, Aliyah, has but one desire: to leave Trenaze's safe boundaries and find the forest that haunts their dreams. After an afternoon of board games in their quiet, sharp-witted company, Horace is ready to follow. They leave with Rumi, an anxious artificer and travelling salesman, in his Wandering Wagon of Wondrous Wares, a semi-sentient self-propelling wagon which always remains safe from Fragments.

Life on the road is filled with quiet hours cooking and cleaning, playing board games with eir companions, or listening to Aliyah's stories of magical worlds. But adventures inevitably find them.

The **first**, at the Dead Archives, a secure waypoint where Horace is once more assaulted by the porcelain-masked figure—an Archivist. They call Aliyah "the Hero", capable of awakening Fragments, and berate em for being too weak to protect them. Horace's skills are immediately tested when Fragments possess dead bodies and attack, and the Wagon's crew barely escapes with their lives.

The **second**, as they seek to cross the Tesrima Ridge, and the pass through the mountain range is flooded. With the help of Keza, an abrasive felnexi who hails from a nearby secret village, they unclog the Fragments-blocked waterways leading to the flood—but their attempt almost takes Rumi's life, and in the process of saving him, Keza reveals her village's existence and is exiled for it. With nowhere to call home anymore, she joins the Wagon crew as they travel to the coastal city of Alleaze.

The **third**, when they arrive there in the middle of the Sea Spirit Festival, and Aliyah is chosen as the Storm Catcher, whose sole purpose is to catch a lightning bolt to re-energize it… and die doing so. They dive into the Bay, knowing the Sea Spirit is another collection of Fragments, and dissipate it before permanently bringing up the lightning rod.

The **fourth** as they sail across the ocean, only for their ship to be destroyed by the kraken—an amalgam of Fragments that stalks Aliyah all the way to the deserted island on which they wash up. They speculate about the nature of Fragments until the Wagon creaks its way into speaking words, and enjoins Aliyah to speak with the Fragments. They obey, and negotiate for the kraken to pull the Wagon and the surviving crew ashore in exchange for Aliyah's listening ear.

The **fifth** as they reach Rumi's home city, Virze, where the very act of creation is revered — and where Rumi had earned a reputation as the Cursed One for his countless mishaps while tinkering. When Keza learns he fled without a word, Keza refuses to leave until he sees his loved ones again. As Rumi makes peace with them, the crew also learns that his inventions are imparted upon him by the Wagon in a creative rush during which he cedes control to it.

From this, Aliyah surmises that the Wagon is in truth a Fragment anchored to a physical body, but the discussion turns sour and it points out they are devoid of light that fills other people unless they have recently absorbed Fragments.

Upset, Aliyah leaves the Wagon. Before Horace can follow, the Archivists capture everyone still in the Wagon, leaving Aliyah behind.

The **sixth** as Aliyah tracks the Archivists to their home base, an ancient city half buried under the mountains, and confronts Archivist Neomi during an experimental ritual targeting Archivist Kol and the Wagon. There, they learn the Archivists view them as a Hero meant to save

Nerezia—and that Horace has always known this. Betrayed and overwhelmed by others' undesired expectations, they lose control of their powers.

Meanwhile, Horace, Keza, and Rumi have successfully escaped their magical cells and explored the city in search of the Wagon, only to discover sleek tunnels full of runic technology not even Rumi can decipher—including a flying machine. When Horace triggers an alarm, they are forced to ride it out of the hangar and above the city, only to spot Aliyah's spread tree form and crash-land near it.

Horace manages to calm Aliyah, and as the Wagon emerges from its ridual-induced torpor, the group makes a daring escape from the city, Archivist Kol in tow. The latter splits from them at the exit, promising to watch over Archivist Neomi despite Horace's insistent invitations to join the party.

With their unity severely tested, the Wagon crew takes a moment to regroup and solidify their bonds before continuing onwards, into the last stretch of their journey towards the forest of Aliyah's dreams.

The pain is so raw, I can barely hold my pen.

The Hero did this to me.

I am … afraid.

Archivist Neomi

1

The Fragment Storm

Life on the Wagon had become more spirited than ever.

Now bestowed with full speech, the Wagon made its presence known not only through moving curtains and opening drawers, but with unceasing use of its low creaking voice. It loved to speak, and relished the use of fancy words Horace had never heard before, especially when it came to complaining, which seemed a top priority to it.

Horace's morning training sessions with Keza earned them regular commentary about their bouts, most of which centred on the irreverent, constant prickling of Keza's claws digging into its wood.

This recrimination had not impressed Keza, who'd promptly informed it "you're my favourite scratching post," to the Wagon's great displeasure. It had extensively lamented the times Keza had been fearful of it and what it could do to her "fragile meat body."

Their frequent arguing reminded Horace of the early days between Keza and Rumi, when every other word held a secret, playful barb. Keza won these exchanges more often than not, but where Rumi had grumbled and stared at Horace in a "you see this?" manner, the Wagon inflicted prolonged gloomy silences upon them all, and there was no escaping its emotions.

It fell to Rumi to save them all from its moodiness, and whenever the Wagon sank into one of its mute grumps, their engineer friend would prompt it with questions on one project or another. Chief amongst them was the broken wing from the dragonfly machine they'd flown—and immediately crashed—through Sioreze. They spent a lot of time talking about weight and buoyancy and gliding, or debating the specific glyphs needed to tell the dragonfly to take to the skies or which direction to move towards. Horace didn't understand any of it, but Rumi's high-pitched rambles and the deep wooden texture of the Wagon's replies formed a strange, comforting melody.

Sometimes, they took a break from the complicated workings of the dragonfly to focus on something far more Horace's speed: wood and fabric panels the Wagon could utilize to communicate numbers and colours with the crew without speaking aloud—a request made by a very grumpy Rumi whose late mornings had been increasingly interrupted by intense games between the Wagon and Aliyah. They built a large panel with three imbedded elements: a ten-faced wheel with numbers, a cube with colours matching the dice, and a near-spherical object with twenty different letters that could be rotated. While Horace helped install those, Aliyah carved numbers and letters along the grid of the saira board to serve as a guide.

Most of the games between Aliyah and the

Wagon happened while Horace was training on the roof with Keza, but e'd had the chance to settle in and watch one. Aliyah sat at the dining table with her board before her, and the Wagon's set slightly to the side. Not a single word crossed her lips as she drafted dice for herself or followed the Wagon's instructions for its play. All Horace had to go on to judge the players' thoughts were her micro expressions and the occasional wave of feelings from the Wagon. Their respective focus was absolute; their silence, oppressive. In a manner of minutes e whispered comments, even if only a casual "oh, the Shield!" before the air in eir lungs exploded in a louder, Rumi-waking form. Games were for chatting, and Horace couldn't have stayed quiet like that. E reserved eir own matches for moments when everyone was awake and willing to hear eir endless happy blathering.

By the time they all settled into their new routines, the Wagon had travelled far northward along the coast, the ocean always peeking on the right, a great blue expanse glittering under the sun. Horace had gotten used to the stingy and refreshing scent of it, brought along by ceaseless winds. They hadn't been without it since Alleaze, and it felt almost impossible to remember eir life *before* the ocean.

Somewhere in the last months, Trenaze had grown into a distant, desertic haze from which only specific memories remained—a friend's laughter, the sweet and acidic taste of tomatoes, the Underlake's cool water as e swam through it, eir mentors' frequent scoldings. It wasn't that Horace didn't remember any of it, but it felt disjointed, fragments of a life e could no longer assemble into a full picture, the glue that was daily routines now lost.

They had gone as far north as they could, however, and the path towards Aliyah's forest led inland. Horace watched the coastline disappear with a pang of regret.

It didn't help that everything grew more difficult.

The nice dirt road stomped on by centuries of occasional travel petered out, and the ground underneath became softer and softer. Within a few days, the windswept plains stilled, tall green grass turning into grey-lilac drooping reeds the farther away from the sea they progressed. Pockets of still water flanked their ever-narrowing path, and before long, standing on top of the Wagon led to a guaranteed assault of bugs of all types. Travel life had transformed from the ethereal beauty of verdant fields and gorgeous blue to a stinky, humid, itchy greyness.

Horace hated it, and Rumi predicted it'd only get worse.

"We can't go around it: our destination's at the centre," he reminded em. "Let's just hope the Fragments behave and steer clear of the Wagon. Every travelling merchant passes stories along about this marsh as a deadly maze of sinking trails in which Fragments are more aggressive than ever. There's a reason no one comes this way."

Only one? Horace thought the growing stench and incessant insects should be added to the list.

Then thick, stifling fog settled over them, increasing the area's oppressing stillness. It was as if the vibrant world outside had slowed and desiccated until even the mosquitoes stopped. Their conversations dropped to hushed tones and Horace spent hours on top of the Wagon alongside Aliyah, surveying the pockets of muddy water for any signs of life. It was pointless, yet it felt like an important solidarity with the Wagon, who was forced to focus on its path rather than animated debates about engineering or Keza's latest offence to its greatness.

The only movement came from Fragments. They drifted past, little beacons of golden light, their sharp edges mellowed by the swirling fog. Like a lantern to guide you, almost inviting, Horace thought. And there were *so many*, all over, their sluggish dance as much part of the scenery as the tall reeds with lilac cattails. They hovered a safe distance from the Wagon, flittering in and out of the fog but never closing in.

Minutes stretched into hours, hours into days. The sun became a faraway memory, its existence flattened into the slow shifting of light. The languid squish of wheels through mud marked their progress, but as they rolled deeper into the swamp, the ground turned more treacherous, repeatedly forcing them to unmire the Wagon before it could continue. In time, Rumi activated its legs and it began to pick its path on the metallic crescents, grumbling every time it made a mistake and sank in.

As the light waned once more, warning of a third impeding night in this never-changing landscape, Horace asked Rumi how long he expected them to need to reach the forest.

"Could be another hour, could be another week. Who knows? I can barely track the passing of time in this cursed place, and I can't tell our pace. It'll take the time it takes."

Rumi clearly disliked the answer as much as Horace did, so e returned to eir bland staring across the marsh from the Wagon's roof. How strange that the land felt as seamless here as the ocean had after weeks sailing on it. The sea at least had frequent winds and an entire crew to help fight the boredom.

When the tiniest breeze stirred through the fog, Horace's heart leaped with hope. Had they finally reached another leg in this journey? Would the infinite marsh come to an end? The wind caressing eir cheek, heralding the advent of a better, less stuffy world, Horace opened the trapdoor and called to eir friends.

"There's a delightful breeze up here!"

Everyone abandoned their activities to enjoy the gusts on top of the Wagon. Keza tilted her face up with a low purr.

"We might yet escape this fog prison," she declared.

To which the Wagon offered a great, unhappy rumble. "I do not like this."

Horace patted the railing. "Oh, come on. Let us have this, won't you? It's just wind."

"It is not *just wind*."

Horace huffed. For all that e loved the Wagon's newfound ability to talk with them effortlessly, it was never satisfied with anything. Paths could be safer, meals could smell better, a joke could be funnier… It provided its criticism with mild benevolence and sometimes balanced them with compliments, but Horace wished its strong opinions trended towards more positive ones. It needed to learn to be less grumpy.

"You're just—"

"The Wagon is correct," Aliyah interrupted with a whisper. "Look at the Fragments."

Horace's stomach dropped as e scanned the surrounding haze for the golden shards. Their slow drift had changed into a rhythmic up and down, their sharp bodies spinning, dragging the fog in their air currents.

"So … they're twirling in the wind? Maybe they're happy about it too!"

"No." Aliyah's tone broke no argument. Her frown deepened the longer she watched. "They're agitated. Excited, maybe, but also … fearful? I—*ah!*"

She grabbed her head in sudden pain, one knee buckling. Horace dove down to hold her shoulders, kneeling beside her as the Wagon swayed forward, almost falling.

"Aliyah, what's going on?"

"Screams…" She panted. "I hear screams. So many of them."

"Huh, everyone?" Rumi squeaked, his small tail swishing around nervously. "I don't think I like this wind either."

The soft breeze that had had them all rush out with joyful excitement had turned into snapping gusts, scattering the fog away. Or rather … sucking it up? Horace's gaze flicked towards the freed horizon and e found emself staring at a wall of fog and Fragments. Dozens—no, hundreds—spun and churned in the great mist. It looked beautiful, a glittering, whirling, and deadly rampart.

And it swept forward, fast, a roiling sandstorm of Fragments engulfing everything on its path. They could never outrun it, even if the Wagon hadn't been struggling.

"Everyone inside!" Keza called.

She yanked Rumi by the collar and sprinted towards the hatch to dump him in. Horace scooped up Aliyah, who hadn't let go of her head and only curled up in a tighter ball. E clambered down, one arm around her, and Keza followed, closing the trapdoor behind her. As soon as she dropped to the ground, she beelined to the front door to lock it.

"Will you be all right, Wagon?" Horace asked.

At first, only the howling of the wind outside answered. Horace's guts twisted. The Wagon had buckled at the same time as Aliyah. Could it hear the Fragments? Was its silence a sign it needed help? But what could they do? The wood around them creaked as Horace sought Rumi's gaze, and the Wagon rattled slow, careful words.

"I would venture that if the Fragments from Archivist Neomi's ritual could not tear my soul from this body, these will not succeed either. However, this promises to be an equally unpleasant experience."

"They're so angry," Aliyah whispered, her voice breaking. "They ... there was ... so much pain."

Horace squeezed her tighter. The Wagon would not be the only one with a miserable time.

They hunkered down in the small living

space, too tense to do much but listen to the howling winds. The metallic screeches of Fragments mingled with them, a horrible grinding sound that set eir teeth on edge. Aliyah leaned into Horace, curled against eir chest, her breaths turning to gasps and hiccups as the Fragments' torment passed through her. It felt like every nightmare she'd ever had, but all at once and far more powerful.

The Wagon rocked around them, pushed by the gusts. Its wood creaked in ways that had nothing with its rhythmic speech, and Horace's stomach squeezed with anxiety as e imagined it battered by a storm of sharp, golden shards. Were those sounds its equivalent of a whimper? Shoulders hunched, eir arms tight around Aliyah, e squeaked an inquiry out.

"Wagon?"

It replied with a full-body shudder that did nothing to assuage Horace's worries and made Rumi flatten his scaled hands on the floor to pat it nervously.

"We're here," he whispered.

From her perch in the rafters, Keza let out an inquisitive *hrm*. "What if we gave it something to listen to? To keep its mind off the screamers out there."

"With what?" Rumi asked. "I doubt it can engage in tricky runic debates right now."

The curtains inside rippled, like a challenge from the Wagon, and Horace couldn't help eir laugh. Even now, tightened down against the onslaught of Fragments, it didn't want to accept it was impaired in any way.

"I had scary stories in mind," Keza said. "It's what we did back home when storms would flood the valley. Hunker down and scare the shit out of each other." She dropped in the middle of the small space and leaned over Rumi. "I bet your pretty little city has the creepiest of them all."

Horace wasn't so sure of that. Out of everything that had happened in their travels, standing under the gaze of the Elders' Council in Keza's village had been one of eir most terrifying experiences. If *that* was their normal, what would their horror stories be like?

"Well ... there's the blanks," Rumi said. "They're creatures entirely devoid of Inspiration that subsist within other people's work—paintings, tapestries, furniture, jewelry—and slowly suck away their lifeforce."

Keza stared at him. "Rumi. Way to *not* build up anything. I didn't even have time to sit down and you're already done!"

He clacked his tongue at her. "Then do it yourself! I'm not a Shaper of Words."

"There's a lake in Trenaze," Horace said, "under the mountain. There are ... stories about its depths."

Keza perched on the back of the nearby couch in one fluid movement, her tail wrapping around her as she turned her full focus to Horace. In eir arms, Aliyah unfurled. Her gaze remained glassy, her brow knitted from pain, but she was paying attention. Eir throat tightened at the sudden pressure. E didn't want to mess it up and make it boring!

"The Underlake is a massive body of water inside Trenaze's mountain. Cast in the eternal shadows of the cave, it's always cool. It's a beloved spot for everyone in the city. Small rafts speckle the lake's surface with soft lanterns, and many go swimming in its waters to fight off the desert heat. It's beautiful, but…"

E let silence stretch after the "but" and an excited thrill hit eir heart when Keza and Rumi leaned in. Horace had spent so many hours listening to Aliyah's stories, getting entranced by them, e had picked up a few tricks.

"There is no explanation for the water in the Underlake. Where does it come from? Where does it go? We do not know."

Horace dropped eir voice into a loud whisper, barely audible above the howling winds and screeching Fragments. Eir heart hammered in eir chest. E knew this story, yet e'd swum countless times in the still waters of the Underlake, these questions far from eir mind.

"They say the lake has no bottom, that it plunges into the earth and never ends, that it has a mind of its own, and if you dive too deep, it speaks to you. They say the whispers are laughter and songs of loved ones, that they wrap around your heart until you have no desire to swim back up. But the lake doesn't take your air. It lets you swim forever, down and down and down, always seeking the distant melodies. And that is how people drown in the Underlake, and why we never find their bodies."

"Creepy," Keza said. "Do you think it's actually bottomless?"

Cold fear ran down Horace's spine as e mumbled. "I never went checking."

"Well you sure won't find *me* swimming that long."

Once, they wouldn't have found her swimming at all. Horace had taught her before they'd embarked on a ship to cross the ocean, and it had always amused em that Keza, who could manipulate the flow of water with her staff and the inherent power of her ancient fighting technique, would rather not touch it whatsoever.

"Was that good? Scary enough?" e asked.

"Unsettling more than terrifying, but I enjoyed that."

"You're weird," Rumi muttered—the first he'd spoken since Horace had finished. He *had* curled in tighter on himself, though, and when he continued, it was in the tones of someone trying very hard to convince himself. "Lakes can't be infinite anyway."

"If you're that sure, you can use that water breather you built Horace to go check."

Keza's cheerfulness only increased when a slight whimper escaped Rumi. She laughed and patted the top of his head.

"My turn. In our village in the valley, when the nights are hot and the stars shine, clouds rise from the Earth. They come spilling out of the mountain in great roiling waves, blanketing our homes until they've grown so thick even the lights of your neighbours are lost to them. The transition is so sudden, it's not rare for people to be caught outside in it. And that, of course, is what the ghosts want."

Horace exchanged a glance with Rumi and was relieved to see the same confusion in his face. "What are ghosts, Keza?"

"Spirits as dangerous as Fragments but unaffected by the Inae techniques. Nothing stops them. They roam through the clouds, hunting for the warmth of the living, because everything around them is as cold as the northern winters. And if they touch you…"

Keza reached across the table, claws out, and every inch of Horace froze as her hand approached.

Then the Wagon buckled.

The floor shifted brutally under them. Horace's lungs, tight with the story's tension, exploded into a surprised cry while Rumi leaped to his feet with a squeal. Although Keza laughed at them, a nervous shakiness filled her chuckles.

"What happened?" she asked.

Horace wished e could run outside to check on the Wagon, but the Fragments howled as strong as ever. If e stepped out in this storm…

A wave of weak reassurance washed over them. It felt strange, for the Wagon's communication to have returned to that stage, but at least it was conscious and speaking to them.

"Right," Horace said aloud, eir voice still shaky from Keza's tale and the sudden change in the Wagon. "Try to give a sign now and then, okay? If there's anything we can do…"

The second wave of reassurance came stronger than the first, setting eir mind a little at ease. E settled back into eir chair. "Well, that rather broke the spell on Keza's story, but I'd like to know what happens to the people trapped with the ghosts."

"If you can find a trail of Inae blooms, it will guide you to a sanctuary within the mountain, so ancient and sacred that not even ghosts can enter it," she said. "If you can't…" She shrugged with exaggerated nonchalance. "Those who have their warmth stolen by ghosts turn to ice, and melt when the clouds lift and the great summer sun pounds on their heads once more."

"Fun!" Rumi all but screamed it, then slapped the deck of Proteins on the table. "I think we should play games now. Maybe the familiarity will help the Wagon."

Not *just* the Wagon, if Horace was to venture

a guess, but they all agreed.

It was more than an hour before the storm abated and they could investigate outside. Yet when Horace wrapped eir hand around the door's handle and pulled, it didn't budge. Frowning, e tried again, to no avail. Was something blocking it, or was the Wagon still holding itself tight, even against Horace?

"Er, Wagon?" e asked.

It hadn't communicated since the brief reassurance, but now it creaked and popped before attempting words. Those emerged as a wooden garbled sound, however, and a powerful wave of embarrassment followed.

"Don't fret it," Horace said, patting the door. "You just had a rough time."

"Might be easier through the top," Keza suggested.

The trapdoor did open, and they had an obvious answer to the issue the moment they stepped outside: the Wagon had sunk into the swamp, mud climbing on its side and covering up the door. Its legs were no longer visible, and when Keza hopped down to get a closer look, her clawed feet sank in. She pulled them out with a loud sucking sound and a pop.

"Somehow I don't think it'll be that easy to extract the Wagon," she said, shaking off the mud from her feet.

"So … we're trapped?" Rumi peeked out from under the top platform's railing, eyes wide with fear and one hand clinging to his Wagon.

"At least the storm's over," Horace said.

Around them, the marsh had returned to its utter stillness, the fog settling over their Wagon and the surrounding plants. No Fragments drifted in and out of the lilac reeds, as if the storm had snatched them all within its winds.

"No victories too small for you, eh?" Rumi said, but he already sounded less distraught about the mud.

"It'll be fine. The Wagon's gonna wake up more, and you and it will create something cool and snazzy that'll drag it right out, and we'll be on our way."

"I can't just build things in a day!"

"Then it'll take a week. It's all right, we're not in any hurry."

"We could be," Keza said. "They're Fragments. Who knows how fast they decide to rile themselves into another storm and bury us for good?"

"I believe we have some time, but not much."

Aliyah had emerged from the Wagon to stand by Rumi's side, her fingers tight around the railing. Deep lines of exhaustion circled her eyes and her shoulders slumped, but she seemed more alert than she had been since the first gusts of wind. Her gaze turned towards the horizon, opposite the direction the storm had rolled in from.

"These Fragments ... they are angry beyond reason. Betrayed to their core, twisted by a suffering they seek to inflict on others. That pain has become their story, and they have no intention of sharing it in peaceful ways. They'll be back, and they'll harm us given the chance. I'm not sure how to stop them, or if I can."

"Fancy that," Rumi muttered. "You'd think

all those horror stories and warnings about the marsh are real."

"Sounds to me like you've got a limited window to work us a miracle, shortscales. Might not wanna waste it in I-told-you-so."

Rumi flicked his tongue out at her before vanishing downstairs—or was it underground now? Inside, at any rate. Horace leaned on the Wagon's side, patting it. "We'll get you out, don't worry. Or you'll get yourself out, most likely. It'll be fine."

E stayed outside. Stiff and swampy as it was, the air helped clear eir mind after hours inside, huddled in the howling winds. The fog curled at eir ankles, wrapping itself around em like a strange blanket, settling in the landscape as if it had never known a lick of wind. It would be easy to forget the danger looming over them, if not for the fear with which Aliyah studied the thick fog.

Sooner or later, the Fragments storm would return, carried across the land by untold pain.

2

A Trail of Blooms

Rumi had snorted in derision when Horace suggested digging out the Wagon, and after an hour of strenuous work with no progress, e was forced to admit he'd been right. Every shovel of mud e threw away was immediately replaced by more, as if the ground had a mind of its own. Aliyah maintained that no Fragments had mixed in with the mud, as they had near Keza's village to block the waterways, but e had a hard time believing it.

"Sorry, buddy," e told the Wagon as e set the shovel aside. "I can try again if Rumi and you don't come up with better."

E did not look forward to it.

At least the Wagon recovered from its ordeal in the storm, and promptly used its voice to complain in depth about the disagreeable sensation of mud clinging to its sleek mechanical legs and the indignity of its current predicament. Real distress lay under the exaggerated whinge, and Horace was glad e had set dough to rise; over the weeks of travel with the Wagon, e'd learned that while it couldn't eat with them, it adored the scent of bread freshly out of the oven. E hoped that'd help soothe its nerves.

Late that night, as Rumi continued debating solutions with the Wagon and Aliyah retired for an early bed, still exhausted from the storm, Horace joined Keza on top of the Wagon. Once the dimmed sunlight was gone, most of the bugs vanished too, leaving em alone with the quiet grey marsh and eir thoughts. Horace didn't have much in the way of brilliant ideas to free the Wagon, but e was ready to push how and when Rumi would tell em. Until then, e wanted to keep watch for another telltale breeze.

A pale blue glow caught eir attention, the only

vibrant colour in the darkening grey-lilac sameness of the marsh. Horace squinted at it until e distinguished a stem growing in small spirals, clinging to the reeds as it climbed upward, ending in a cluster of leaves wrapped around the blue light. As Horace watched, the leaves unfurled from their protective sphere, revealing a beautiful, bulbous flower.

"Keza, look!" It was so at odds with the rest of the swamp, delicate and colourful. "Just like your stories."

"Horace… That's *exactly* like the stories."

Awe filled her voice and she leaped down from the Wagon, landing into the muddy surroundings with a slight squish.

"What?" Horace's gaze returned to the plant and e squinted. It had been months since e'd seen the strange vines inside the Inari Pass and along the path to Keza's village, but these did look awfully similar. "Wait, Keza!"

She was already halfway to it, picking her way across the treacherous grounds, but she paused and turned. "These are Inae blooms, Horace."

Keza approached the plant with slow reverence. Its tallest flower rested at her eye level and she lifted it with the tip of her claw. Despite the fog half concealing her, Horace caught the sadness flittering in her expression. Her tail flicked, and she turned her gaze to her surroundings. In a matter of seconds, she let out a satisfied "Ah!" and dove deeper into the marsh.

"Keza!"

Horace scrambled down the side of the Wagon and hurried after her. Eir boots sucked into the mud and e had to fight for every stride, but soon e found her again, standing by a new flower, her outline barely visible.

"You can't go running off like that," e said. "You'll get lost!"

Her back arched as she turned towards em, smirking. "These flowers *are* guides. They'll lead me where I need to be, and back. I can already see the next one."

Her tail flicked with pure mischief and she darted off again, dashing to the next bloom.

Horace sprinted after her, picking eir path through the marsh. Eir boots squished with every step, but e didn't sink in the mud, nor did the ground collapse under eir weight to plunge em knee-deep in water. The flowers had grown along a line of packed dirt, always barely in sight of one another, a trail of tiny blue lights in a world of fog.

The Wagon had long since vanished behind them, and the further Horace got, the tighter eir chest compressed. But every time e thought of returning, e glimpsed of Keza ahead—a flick of her tail, an outline—and e couldn't abandon her, not to a marsh full of resentful Fragments, not on the strength of an old legend.

"Keza, wait!" e called again, and this time she did stop, allowing em to catch up. E stopped by her, hands on eir thighs as e gasped for breath. "We could at least walk it together."

"I hadn't heard you following." Her tail wrapped around her leg and a tightness slipped in her voice as she added. "You shouldn't have."

E stopped short. "What?"

"You *shouldn't have*." Her ears flattened as she turned to em. "The last time you followed me back to an Inae tribe, I was exiled. These guides are for *us*, knowledge passed since ages lost. Why would these people be any less secretive than my own? They might not welcome you."

They might not welcome Keza, either. Horace kept the retort to emself; she knew this, and that fear was behind her anger now. E could pretend e didn't understand that and let her vent on em.

"You darted off without warning and this place is dangerous," e said instead. "I know you're strong, but I don't think any of us should venture out alone. I want to be there. I want to support you."

Her tail loosened and her ears perked as she relaxed. "You're sweet, Horace, but I can handle myself."

"You shouldn't have to." E crossed eir arms. "It's not how we do things. We're your second family now, remember?"

Keza rolled her eyes with a breezy, I-give-up laugh. "You're a stubborn, overfriendly pest," she said with utmost love, "so fine, I suppose you can tag along. It might help to have someone give them all big puppy eyes and a friendly grin so they don't throw us out immediately." Her gaze latched onto the next Inae bloom and she started off. "Hopefully the Wagon knows what to tell the others about our disappearance."

Horace puffed out eir chest and responded in eir best imitation of the deep, creaking voice. "Foolhardy, reckless little hunks of flesh ran into the fog, heedless of the dangers, putting all of their faith in the power of stories."

Keza snorted. "You've been listening to it too much."

They trekked on mostly in silence, speaking only to warn of sinking puddles or to point out the next flower on their trail. Before long, a friendly competition emerged between them, each attempting to spot the soft hue of the Inae blooms before the other. Keza won most of the time, her sharp eyes better at piercing the fog-shrouded reeds in the dark. With the sun gone, Horace could barely pick eir path through the marsh.

Fragments eventually returned, drifting through the surrounding mists with the same laziness they'd initially had, golden lanterns in the shadows. More than once, one of them spun until it emitted a low, screeching buzz, before diving towards them. Keza swiped her staff out, knocking it off course with a quick sweep. As long as the Fragments didn't coordinate an attack, they would be fine, but Horace feared the slightest gust of wind. If another storm brewed, they wouldn't have the Wagon to hide in.

After an hour—or three, who knew, really?—of this near-silent trek, Horace needed to break the hush.

"So ... you think you'll find your people there?" e asked.

Keza started at eir voice. Her claws dug into the ground, and her tail swished through the air in quick movements. For all of her pretend cool, she was as tense as e was.

"My tribe spent centuries isolated from the world. We're resourceful and secretive. Is it so hard to believe a sister group exists here?"

"... No? Maybe? I don't know! Your people lived in a beautiful nestled valley with water aqueducts and terrace farming and gorgeous trees. It was idyllic!"

More importantly, it was not a deadly swamp worryingly devoid of any typical animal life. Shouldn't frogs be eating the mosquitoes or something?

Keza's ears flicked down, and she didn't reply to em as she moved forward. Horace followed with a sigh. Ever since she'd admitted to missing her kittens on the slopes near Sioreze, e'd tried to broach the topic of her home a handful of times. E didn't like that she suffered in silence, but Keza always shut down those conversations. E'd asked Rumi if she was more open with him, and he'd answered that apart from that long night in a cell, it was as though her children didn't exist.

Horace was still trying very hard to think of ways to say "talk to me about your kittens" or "why did your people hide from the world?" when the patterns of Inae blooms changed. Instead of one, they could spot three blue flowers, and then six, and finally a dozen—but those were no longer on the ground: they had scaled the wall of a large structure rising out of the fog.

Horace craned eir neck as e took in the new sight. The wall curved in a hexagonal shape and the shadow of a dome lingered through the dark. Thick columns marked each corner, and swooping lines had been carved within them. The flowers' vines used them as furrows, climbing upward and illuminating the building with pockets of blue glow. The style reminded em of the tunnels in the Inari Pass, especially towards the bottom of the columns where the rounded lines turned into blocky, geometrical patterns.

An arched gateway commanded attention in the middle of the wall, its lines at angles rather than describing a smooth curve, the whole of which formed a perfect hexagon. Figures had been carved in a variety of strange positions along its top, and two heavy doors barred the way under them. Horace trudged up to the gate and was relieved when eir boots found harder ground and stopped squishing with every step. When e didn't spot a knocker, e rapped eir knuckles onto the dark wood and called out.

"HELLO? We're friends!"

Eir only answer was Keza's stifled but horrified laugh behind em. "Horace! Even if anyone's here, they won't open to you knocking."

"They would if they were polite."

"You don't stay hidden by welcoming every visitor. Besides, I know how to open this." As Horace returned to her side, she pointed at the carved figures with her staff. "I've seen something like those before."

She centred herself in front of the depictions then brought her staff down to mimic the first position, legs spread apart and weapon horizontally before her. From there, Keza moved to the second image, her staff and body transitioning in one graceful motion. Her entire being spun about between stances as she followed the sequence depicted above, half dance and half training routine, and power built as her staff swished through air, a pressure in eir ears and chest. She repeated the process, over and over, the succession ever more fluid, the steps less defined as she chained them with increasing ease. Around her, the marsh water slid out of its puddles to mimic the dance.

To Horace, it was as breathtaking as the first day e'd seen Keza's routines. The door, however, did not budge.

After another gruelling cycle of repetitions with no response, Keza stopped, her chest heaving. The water splashed to the ground and the power built up vanished, making Horace's ears pop with the pressure change.

"Maybe I was wrong…" she said.

There was a sharp edge to Keza's tone, a blade she might cut herself on. It made Horace's stomach knot itself up very tight, and e blurted out "No, I felt it! Maybe it's just a little off."

She turned a challenging glare on em.

"It's, hum…"

Now e needed to find *how* it was off. E raked eir

brain, thinking of the countless times e'd seen her go through similar exercises. The positions had been different, then, more of a dancing equilibrium between body and staff, a routine meant to be always moving, circling, going high and low. These little images carved into the arch… They were squared, two feet on the ground, stable. The kind e would have an easier time with.

"Maybe it's your transitions?" e ventured. "You transfer between the poses like you would between yours."

Her tail flicked and her fur puffed. Fear spiked through Horace at Keza's frown. Countless mentors had mocked em for eir thoughts before, and she obviously disagreed.

"Horace, I am a *master* at this technique," she said, gritting out the words and giving her staff a quick spin.

"At-at *yours*!" e squeaked out. "Yours, from your village, where it's all wooshy and splashy, but these are … brutish?"

E mimicked the position one by one, puffing out eir chest and making a grunt sound. Keza's nose twitched as she suppressed a laugh, but she returned her attention to the markings above the door, all sharp lines and right angles, studying them with renewed interest. Relief washed over Horace, leaving em light-headed and warm. She was listening to em, taking eir opinions seriously. In time, her ears twitched and she released a questioning *mrow*.

"I see your point. Brutish. I wonder if…"

Keza stepped back into her position under the arch, and settled into the first stance, legs spread out and staff held horizontally between both hands. With a slow and deep inhale, she launched herself into the sequence again.

This time, however, she transitioned with sharp movements, shoving all of her strength into brutal swings of her staff, landing heavily. It took her several loops through the positions to wean out the fluid swoops that belonged to her natural technique, but with every pass her swings became more forceful, her transfer between one stance and the next more sudden. The *thwack* of her staff slicing the air punctuated every switch.

A thrumming power built in the marsh and the geometrical carvings along the gate lit up, a soft lavender hue that melded within the bloom's blue light. The glow climbed in cadence with Keza's dance, bringing new life to the structure. Grime marred once-pale walls and time had smoothed many of its corners, yet the stony ruins retained an aura of grandeur that had Horace gaping.

In front of em, Keza moved through the last transition, leaping up and smashing her staff down to the ground, digging it deep into the mud as her feet braced her on each side of it. The *thud* of her landing echoed through the marsh, a force of its own.

A deep gong answered, the sound vibrating through Horace's lungs and chest. The great doors cracked open along the pale lilac lines, splitting in several chunks that slid either into the walls, or inward.

With a satisfied smile, Keza straightened up, yanked her staff out of the ground, and flicked the mud off it.

"Seems we're welcome after all, big fella."

3

Trainees and Master

No one greeted them inside the ancient building. They stalked through empty corridors, passing unidentifiable rooms with broken furniture. There had been a dormitory and a kitchen, of that Horace was certain from the leftover bed frames and clay ovens, but the rest remained a mystery.

It didn't help that they navigated without proper light, using the starlight provided by rare cracks in the walls and surviving windows or by the occasional blue glow of trailing Inae blooms. E kept stubbing eir toes on unseen stones, and after the second hiss of pain, Keza shushed em.

"I hear something," she whispered.

Light reflected off her eyes like mirrors. It

reminded Horace of the Elders in her village, their bodies concealed by the foliage but their eyes clearly visible. It had been creepy then, and it was now, too. It didn't help that even straining to listen, Horace didn't hear anything.

"Are you sure?" Despite eir best efforts, eir voice bounced off the nearby walls, and e hunched eir shoulders at it.

"Follow me and soon enough you'll be sure yourself."

She was right. They stalked farther down the corridor, and e picked up on a distant, rhythmic echo. It felt familiar, objects hitting one another, though e couldn't place exactly what. Keza's strides lengthened, and so did eirs, curiosity overtaking any sort of prudence. They had followed the trail of Inae blooms through the dangerous marsh for a chance to meet more of Keza's people, and it sounded like they would get their wish.

The deeper they made it in, the clearer the noise became, a metronomic *thwack* that had Horace's feet curling in anticipation. Then they emerged into a wide inner court, the muddy ground overtaken by lilac reeds at least three metres high, and the source of came into view.

Eight figures moved in pairs at the centre, their stout bodies half as tall as the reeds, built out of earth and drooping with mud. The latter linked their arms together into a solid object—a *staff*—and they swept at each other, striking and parrying, darting in and out of battle with sudden and powerful maneuvers. Training, Horace realized. Under the moonlight and diffuse blue from blooms clinging along the walls, their clashes were an eerie spectacle and Horace couldn't help the fascinated "wow" that escaped eir lips.

The eight fighters whirled on em in one synchronized jump, abandoning their sparring without second thought.

"Oh, Horace," Keza muttered, bringing her staff into ready position and dropping into a fighting stance.

"They could be friendly?"

But even as e said it, a discordant metallic

screech rose from the creatures, the familiar and terrifying sound of angry Fragments.

"Then again, maybe not."

Horace scrambled to get eir sword and shield up as the group rushed them.

E barely stopped the first blow. A tight knot lodged itself in eir throat as another came, then a third. E blocked and parried, falling into the rhythm of the sudden battle, eir body moved by instincts honed through Keza's training.

Three of the trainees surrounded em, their staves filed to a point, but their maneuvers felt slow, predictable. Was something wrong with them? E stopped blows with surprising ease, eir feet sliding against the ground to readjust eir balance and absorb the force behind them. Then e caught from the corner of eir eyes the whirlwind of spinning, dancing staff that was Keza, and e understood: e had been training against a much faster opponent, and it was paying off.

Horace plunged into the fight with renewed vigour, catching the spear stabs with eir shield, sidestepping attacks or blocking them with eir sword. Only the trainees' superior number forced em on the defensive, all of eir energy spent staving off the trio instead of preparing eir strikes. E had gotten *way* better since meeting Keza, but not yet quite good enough to destroy three opponents at once.

Slowly, one step at a time, Horace brought emself closer to Keza, keeping eir teammate at eir back.

"Wanna trade?" she asked, her grin clear from her upbeat tone. She had the remaining five trainees jabbing at her, but she sounded like she was enjoying herself.

"No, thank you, I'm good!" Horace replied, eir breath short from the constant work batting away one strike or another. "I could use a moment's distraction if you've got it."

She laughed. "I like a challenge. Be ready to jump on my say-so."

Jump? Horace stifled eir confusion and focused on holding eir own. E couldn't watch Keza, but e felt her leave eir back, and the rapid succession of *thwacks* as she brutalized the five mud trainees around her told em all e needed. Eir ears thrummed with the rising ambient power of her technique. When she landed back right behind em, her tail brushing against eir thighs, eir entire muscles tensed for her signal.

"Jump!" she called.

E obeyed, leaping as far up as e could. Her staff swept under em in a wide circle, and with it came a wave of force, as if the weapon itself had extended farther. It hit the three trainees' legs, and muddy water flew out of their limbs, leaving behind thick pillars of crumbling dried earth and a hint of the single golden shard beneath. Horace dived forward the instant eir feet touched the ground, smashing one trainee in the face with eir shield while e plunged eir sword in the second's chest.

The blade sank into the mud, nice and deadly, but when Horace tried to yank it back, it resisted. Shock and confusion stalled em, and that fraction of a moment between eir pull and eir sword releasing from the pressure was all the third trainee needed. Its spear dug into Horace's shoulder and the spurt of pain made em stumble.

Every motion practised countless times, his body moves in sudden bursts. The Mountain to the Bridge to the Wall. The Wall—hold the Wall. He has to hold the Wall, one of eight pillars, and force this pull to go through him even if it tears him apart. No matter what, he has to protect the master. Agony unravels him from the inside-outside, pulling and pulling. He screams as his knees buckle, a fracture in the wall. No, no. He has to hold it, this last line of defence—a worthy sacrifice.

The vision receded as the ground rushed up to meet Horace. E threw eir arms up and hit it hard, then rolled to the side in case another strike was coming for em. Gritting eir teeth against the pain throbbing in eir shoulder, e scrambled back to eir feet and tried to regain eir bearings. E'd dropped eir sword, but eir shield had thankfully stayed strapped to eir arm. The opponent e'd smashed it in had lost huge swathes of dried earth, revealing amorphous golden light underneath, but the two others seemed fine.

Keza was still fighting most of her own mud trainees, but half of them had partly turned into cracked earth. She jumped above a jab forward and spun her staff midair, landing with a wide sweep towards the covered Fragments. Water spouted out of them as she connected the strike, some splashing on the ground, and more following the arc of her staff to fly off in a different direction. She followed up with two quick hits from the butt of her staff, sending chunks of dirt spraying, tearing down the body to reveal the Fragment shard embedded within. It stopped moving once exposed, as if stunned by its change of state.

Neat, Horace thought, except e couldn't do that. At least not the first, drying step. Eir three opponents had very brittle legs now, and e could smash those as well as anyone.

But first, e needed eir sword back. It had half sunk into the mud, and eir three trainees stood between it and Horace. Shield at the ready, e baited them away from the sword, slowly circling, letting them get close enough for an occasional strike. They weren't fast, and once e'd created distance, Horace dashed for eir weapon and scooped it up. Eir wounded shoulder throbbed from the sudden movements, but the crunch of earth behind warned em e had no time to recoup from the pain. E spun and raised eir shield, catching the spear aimed at eir back.

The back and forth cadence of battle returned, and although it was familiar from months of training, the pain shooting through Horace's shoulder every time e parried was a stark reminder of the deadlier stakes.

At the first opportunity, e dropped into a crouch and kicked at one of the trainee's legs. Earth chunks flew about and it stumbled, one of its legs gone. Horace blocked an incoming attack from another and sprang back, putting some distance between em and the fallen mud trainee. With only two left to deal with, e had an easier time weaving between their defences, ignoring the still-muddy upper part of their body to hack and smash at their dried-out legs, chipping away at them until they'd grown unstable. When e tried to bash one in the face with eir shield, however, the mud reformed over the Fragments. This wasn't a job e could finish on eir own.

Perhaps it was time to take up Keza on her earlier offer.

When e glanced back, Keza had only two of her trainees left. The rest floated, minuscule Fragment shards—much smaller than Horace had ever seen, barely the size of eir hands. A pang of guilt coursed through em; they looked so defenceless. They had already proven that to be a lie, however.

"Keza, trade you a few?" e asked.

Her sharp chuckle warmed eir heart. "Knew you'd change your mind."

She forced her remaining opponents back with a wide sweep, and in the brief opening, they ran to each other's group. Horace sprinted in shield first, swinging the heavy piece of metal at the leftmost trainee and dusting most of it in a single blow. The second one tried to use the opportunity to strike, but Horace knocked the blow away with eir sword. The jolt coursed all the way up to eir wounded shoulder, dragging a hiss out of em. Best not to think about how awful it'd all feel once adrenaline wore out, and keep on fighting.

Between the two of them, they made short work of the remaining trainees, hacking and slamming away the rest of the earth until it lay scattered in the courtyard, leaving behind only the floating shards. Despite the non-existent light, their glow was barely perceptible and the pinpricks of gold felt distinctly *confused* to Horace—as if they didn't know what to do now that their connection to the earth had been broken.

Keza ignored them all and ran to eir side. "You're hurt."

Sweat coated eir body from the exertion, eir curled hair stuck to eir forehead, eir lungs burned and the wound stung fiercely, but Horace grinned at her, eir heart still full of pride from that battle. E had held eir own in a fight!

"Nothing a bit of bandage can't fix."

"Horace, I can see the blood stain spreading.

Sit your ass down and put some pressure on it."

E dropped to the ground with a huff and searched for a handkerchief to press onto the gash. No sense in arguing with Keza, especially when she was right to begin with. Besides, e didn't want the wound to get worse. What if it limited eir arm movement and e couldn't cook for a while? The Wagon had shared horrifying tales of what Rumi used to eat on his own, and Horace refused to experience *that*.

Keza was bending over em to take a look when the Fragments they'd left floating all suddenly twirled on themselves before drifting towards the centre of a small stone dais, raised a foot above the muddy ground and free of it. Three hovered in the middle of that space while the others arranged themselves around, forming an almost star-shaped pattern: one above, one on each side, and two below. Their meagre light linked and grew, extending towards one another but also outward until the shape became far more familiar than a star.

It was a person, stout and small, all golden

glow but for the eight shards forming its body, spinning and no longer confused. It turned its head towards them with a low screech of metal.

"Ominous, eh?" Horace muttered, clambering back up but keeping a hand over eir wound.

A long staff appeared in the fragmented figure's hands in response.

"Very," Keza whispered, bringing her own weapon at the ready.

It was all she had time for. The figure surged forward with lightning speed, closing the distance between them in the blink of an eye. One moment it was on the dais, the next its staff *thwacked* against Keza's, startling Horace backward. That strike had been aimed for eir skull, and it would have cracked it had Keza not caught it. She kept her weapon horizontal above her head, her arms trembling with the effort of holding it back. The figure screeched, filling the courtyard with its discordant scraping before redoubling its assault on her.

They moved in a flurry, Keza a spinning and

bending wave of dodging, the Fragment figure a brutal and solid attacker, its two feet never leaving the ground as she danced around him, trying to find an opening. Horace could only stare as the air vibrated with the rhythm of their battle and crackled with power. Sometimes, e sensed the waves of force inherent to Keza's technique—the ones that had displaced Fragments so often, serving as a shield as much as a weapon—but every time she slung one towards her opponent, the figure adopted a defensive stance, legs widespread, and smashed its staff into the ground to intercept and dispel it.

Horace couldn't have said how long the fight lasted. E tried to stay focused and keep eir shield at the ready—to stay alert for an opportunity to help, as e had when they had escaped Sioreze—but e grew more lightheaded by the second. Eir handkerchief had gotten soaked with blood. Like their shirt. Oh. E swayed at the sight of it and blinked out a wave of encroaching darkness.

In that second of distraction, the figure shoved Keza back and rushed em. She was on top of it in an instant, smacking its first strike at Horace to the side, but the last-minute catch had put her off balance. With a sharp hit of its stone staff, it swept her off her feet and rammed the butt of it in her chest. She gasped, her breath turning into a wheeze.

Fear shot through Horace as the figure lifted its staff to strike again. It was eir weakness that had forced her to rush, and e refused to let that be the end of it. E rushed forward, shield raised, and slammed into the figure before it could strike Keza again. The Fragment shrieked, an ear-bleeding screech of metal, and as they hit the ground, one of the legs sliced through eir shin.

A body. A voice.

The overpowering thoughts filled eir mind, leaving em dazed. Pure craving tugged at eir heart, the Fragments' desire so potent that Horace forgot to breathe, forgot emself entirely. The courtyard changed before eir eyes, wild reeds vanishing to as a beautiful floor with geometric patterns in maize and blue surrounding the middle dais. Two fighters circled each other upon it, but Horace blinked it all away, forcing eir mind not to wander and give in. The reward for eir effort was a splitting headache.

"*Cede your body,*" the shrieking, metallic voice burst in eir head. "*It is ours. It is mine.*"

No! Panic swelled through em as e fought the pressure, but the floor returned and the rhythmic *thwack* of staves echoed in eir mind.

"Horace? Horace!" Keza's voice. So distant now. Something pricked eir shoulder. Her claws? "Snap out of it!"

"*Give in. We **must** teach.*"

The urgency of the Fragments' demands threatened to drown em. This amalgam had such a raw desire to *be*, it washed everything else away. But there had been a hint of story there, a goal, something *not em* to cling to as distinct. Aliyah often described her appeasement of Fragments as listening to them, giving their tale a home or a chance to be told. Maybe…

"Teach?" e asked—and e had no idea if e spoke it aloud, or if the words drifted in eir mind.

"The earth resolve is sacred to Inae. It cannot be lost." The urgency of its tone remained, but the pressure lessened—a deep force hovering at the ready. *"She will do, water that she is. She must."*

Eir vision cleared, grey-lilac reeds returning into focus. E was kneeling on the ground, but e couldn't feel it. E couldn't feel much beyond eir overwhelming headache. The person-shaped amalgam of Fragments was nowhere around. Had it all sunk into em?

"Keza..." e gasped. "It's your people—an Inae Master, I think? Do you... Do you want to learn ... its fighting technique?"

E was slipping again, eir vision blurring, and the Fragment spilled words from eir lips, each like a shard in eir mouth. "Master of the Water Dance, we seek to bestow the strength of the mountain on you."

It was eir voice, distorted and angry. Horace clenched eir hand. Relief mixed with eir panic when it responded, eir fingers curling into the mud.

"Do that without my friend," she snapped back. "This is some creepy shit."

"No," it rumbled.

Horace yanked control back of eir body. The Inae Master's presence was an endless pressure, the pain of it growing by the second. E could barely think through its overpowering need to teach Keza, eir own desires mixing in until e struggled to draw a line between the two.

Keza had come here for this. She'd wanted to connect with her people, she deserved to do so, and e was the reason she couldn't to begin with.

"I'll do it," e said. "I'll let you in, but not—" Horace gasped as powerful glee coursed through em and the Inae Master pressed itself deeper in eir consciousness. E was slipping so quickly, darkness encroaching. The pain, the intense emotions that weren't eirs … it was overwhelming. E gritted eir teeth. "This is a lending arrangement. It's *my* body and I want it back."

"Horace, don't do this."

"When your teaching is done," Horace continued, ignoring Keza, "we know someone who can help you. She can … free you and yours."

There was no hesitation, only a powerful sense of agreement and a renewed pressure. It'd have to be good enough. E had to trust this Fragment would release em go when its story was told, that it wasn't malicious like the others in this marsh. Horace let go of eir body. Eir vision faltered and the dark ground turned into a sun-blessed floor, memories not eir own filling eir mind.

4

On Muddy Grounds

Keza hated everything about this.

She could pinpoint the exact moment Horace lost control. Eir pained smile turned into a hard grimace, the joy vanished from eir gaze, and eir head snapped up to glare at her. Same body, but this jerk looked nothing like the original. It didn't even speak the same, every word a punch through the air instead of an invitation.

"Finally."

It rolled eir shoulders before lumbering up and crossing eir arms. Horace had never looked this haughty, and Keza twitched with the urge to punch it in the face.

"Unfortunate that this body is wounded, but

you can begin while I let it rest. Your first task is to stand immobile until I wake up. I will know if you move, so do not think to reassume your position as the sun rises."

"I've not agreed to any of this shit," she snapped. "Get out of there."

"I have been welcomed in."

Yeah, *right.* As if Keza hadn't seen Horace fight for every inch of control in the last few minutes. Just because this asshole had bullied its way into her friend's body didn't mean she had to play along. She thunked her staff to the ground and leaned on it, as nonchalant as she could.

"I'm not buying it."

"It matters not. It is what it is. Your refusal to participate only prolongs eir possession and wastes eir sacrifice."

Keza's fur puffed as guilt welled up within her. It was baiting her, and it was working. She wanted to bash it out of Horace, and she hissed at it in warning. This amused it, a condescending expression totally foreign on Horace's soft traits.

"Do you not wish to learn?" it asked. "You are not an ideal pupil, fickle and spiteful as you are, but I am willing to overlook those flaws. You should understand that our art *must* be preserved. Or have our water brethren fallen so low that you'd refuse the teachings of an Inae Master?"

Keza swiped her staff up with an angry spin, dropping into a fighting stance with another hiss. It could needle *her* as much as it wanted—she knew her own worth—but to slight the rest of her people? Only she got to do that.

"Were you an Elder, by any chance? You're just as pissy and arrogant as those back home."

"I was."

Its flat tone sent thick cords of unease running down her spine. Horace had been *terrified* of the Elders lurking in the trees, the night of her exile. All this shit would be strange enough if she'd been talking to a floating Fragment, but through em? She hated it. Then it made it worse by bowing to her, however briefly.

"I am Elder Nerevin, they/them—the

youngest of the three, and the only Inae Master. My colleagues also used to call me arrogant, though they preferred 'abrasive' to 'pissy'."

Turned out Elders were a pain in the ass everywhere. Keza hated how that made this Nerevin more relatable.

"Pissy's better," she declared, loosening up her posture to take a quick bow. "Keza Nesmit, she/her. The one who crossed an entire ocean to be called fickle and spiteful by the same kind of assholes we had at home, apparently."

Nerevin snorted. For all that they had Horace's body and voice, Keza couldn't unsee the other person residing within—how with a cock of their head, they covered part of their face with Horace's curls, or how they seemed smaller and wider, holding themself closer to the ground, legs always perfectly placed, ready to spring into action. Horace had made a lot of progress over time—e was a proper fighter now, eir reflexes and battle awareness strong enough to last against her most mornings—but e didn't carry emself like a martial expert. To Horace, fighting was a means to protect loved ones; to Nerevin, it was a way of being, inscribed in their soul.

"Will you learn, then?" they asked, a hush to their tone that bordered on pleading.

She still wanted to spurn them. Even knowing Horace most likely *had* welcomed the Fragment in, the self-sacrificing fool, and even acknowledging the yearning growing with every instant talking to them, studying their pose, absorbing the sheer skill they exuded... Keza wanted to say no. On principle. They *had* possessed one of her best friends and it had looked painful as shit.

"Only if you respect your word and take care of eir body," she grudgingly agreed. "Give em eir rest, bandage that wound, and release em when we're done, or I'm shoving you out of there and leaving with Horace."

Nerevin lifted a doubtful eyebrow but did not dispute her ability to do so.

"Then you will stand immobile until my return, as requested."

Vicious condescension oozed from their tone, and by the stars she wanted to smack them so badly—just one quick punch, for her own sanity.

"Is that an actual lesson, or are you just getting off the perceived authority?"

A slow smile curled their lips. "A little of both, perhaps. It is a test of discipline and endurance. If I quite enjoy putting students through it, that is but incidental."

She rolled her eyes, and in the instant she stopped looking directly at Nerevin, a long staff of rock materialized in their hands. They tapped her feet with it, nudging them into position, farther apart than she was used to.

"I shall return once this body has recovered," they declared.

They walked away without another word, and Keza's first real test was to stay put instead of dashing after them to make sure they didn't *leave* with Horace's body. It sounded like they— this *collection of Fragments*—did want to teach her. She remembered sitting for hours in a running stream, letting the water flow "through" her. Maybe she was lucky Elder Nerevin hadn't buried her halfway in the mud.

She gritted her teeth as Horace's form exited through the courtyard's broken archway and vanished, and prayed to the stars that their joint trust in this Fragment wasn't misplaced. If it was, though, there wouldn't be a corner of this world recluse enough to spare Nerevin from her wrath.

Nerevin left her standing there for an eternity.

The sun rose somewhere through all the fog, and after that it was impossible to tell how much time passed in the sameness of the grey. Only the ache ebbing in and out of her muscles, from unbearable to unnoticeable in cycles, and her growing pit of hunger marked the hours. It trickled by until she stopped perceiving it. Her mind and body moved past exhaustion, past hunger, leaving her only a statue in the courtyard.

Something small and sharp flicked at the edge

of her vision. Flying at her. Keza's reflexes kicked in and she bent backward, sidestepping at the same time, and the narrow rock hurtled less than an inch past her face, landing in the mud with a distant plop.

Pain clenched her muscles at the sudden motion, and when her feet hit the ground to catch herself, her entire body went rigid in protest. She hadn't moved in hours, and now she did this? It wasn't having it. Keza lost her balance with a hiss and fell in the mud, her staff digging into her shoulders at the impact.

Elder Nerevin strode closer to loom over her, hands clasped behind their back. Their sneer doused the reflexive flicker of warmth at seeing Horace.

"I told you not to move," they said.

"Not until your return," she countered. "You're back now, aren't you?"

Their lips twitched into a brief smile, then they offered a hand to help her up. Horace had done the same so often that she grabbed their wrist without hesitation. Elder Nerevin did not pull her. Their fingers dug into her battered muscles, prodding them here and there, and they clacked their tongue.

"Not too bad."

They dropped her, slipping their arm out of her grip so she'd fall. Keza gritted her teeth, arching her back enough to slam her palms in the ground and backflip up, ignoring the protest of her screaming body at the supple jump. She refused to *lumber* to her feet for their amusement.

"You're an asshole," she stated, because it was true and because she needed to hear it aloud, to remind herself they weren't friends even if they lived in Horace's body. "You gonna at least explain what all that standing still was for?"

"Of course. I *am* here to teach, after all," they said.

Keza's tail flicked in annoyance, but she bit down on her snark. Nerevin had already proven they enjoyed getting a rise out of her and she didn't want to give them the satisfaction.

"To acquire the prowess of mountains, you

must learn to move as one. The earth can change in fast and shattering ways, but it otherwise shapes itself through slow and subtle processes spanning millennia or more. Its core strength is stability. A mountain would have let the rock hit it without flinching."

This time, she couldn't help her bitter laugh. "So you *did* want me to stand there and eat shit."

"Want, yes," they conceded. "Expected you to, no. Water is never still. Even the ocean has broad currents."

"Or I just didn't want to get smashed in the face by a rock."

Nerevin did not acknowledge that. They crouched down and placed their palm on the ground, and when they lifted their hand a long stone staff followed.

"Are you ready to begin, Keza Nesmit?"

Her entire body ached. She had neither slept nor eaten in a full day, and the world was starting to feel one step removed and fuzzy. She lived on instinct and shifting moods, and any of her old mentors would've sent her home to rest.

But Nerevin was not them; they had their own methods, and although they enjoyed the brutality of them too much for her liking, she'd give them a chance. Horace had bought her time with an Inae Master at deep risk to eirself, and despite all her misgivings about it, she could not flaunt the opportunity to touch her home again, to learn more of her people, even if from a different time and place.

She brought her staff to bear, the familiar grip anchoring her.

"Always."

Nerevin tapped her heels with their staff, shifting her feet back to how they had spent the last hours. Her muscles screamed at this return, and she worried they'd lock into place before whatever came next.

"Keep one foot touching the ground at all times," they said, "and don't let me hit you."

It was the only warning Keza received before they swung the stone staff at her. Her instincts took over and she leaped aside, dodging the strike. As her mistake sank in and she cursed,

Nerevin smacked her right foot with the staff in reproach.

"Don't jump. Surely you can manage that much."

Keza growled at them, but when they launched into another series of attacks, her feet remained firmly on the ground—or one of them, at least. She hated being cut off from her usual mix of leaps, sidesteps, and twirls. Sure, one foot on the ground allowed for some flexible dodging, but for the most part she was forced to intercept Nerevin's strikes with her own. The Inae Master put tremendous strength behind their assault, and her arms trembled with each impact. More than once, the shock threw her off her feet—and then Nerevin jabbed her ankle again, as though the crime was on par with jumping out of the way.

Hours passed in ceaseless training, and though the light remained the same dim grey, Keza could've sworn they'd reached noon. Her muscles ached from the constant battering and drawn-out night of immobility, and the pain spasmed down her arms with every new blow. Every time she fell, she pushed herself up again. Dried mud caked her clothes and fur; she was more pain than person, but she wouldn't give up.

And she was learning.

She was holding her own in the bouts for longer. Her feet kept to the ground, moving only to redistribute weight and keep her balance as she rose her staff to deflect or catch an attack. It felt strange, to move so little, to contain herself to subtle shifts, but it helped her focus on the directions the blows came from, the strength of her arms, and the way her body could support them.

Then Nerevin smashed their staff into hers so hard, her foot slipped through the mud. Darkness washed over her as she hit the ground, the world blinking out for a moment. Had it been a second? Ten? It was too long for her to ignore. She sat up, but did not rise to her feet.

"I need to stop and rest."

Nerevin scowled at her request, but Horace's hand gripped the staff tightly and they were leaning on it. A minute ago, she would've sworn she'd caught them swaying. She hadn't dreamt it.

"So do you. Have you even eaten? You have a body to care for now."

"Evidently," they replied, lips thinning into a displeased line. "I suppose that will be enough for the day. You *have* made considerable progress."

Keza did her best to hide the wave of pride rushing to her head, but her tail gave happy swishes that didn't go unnoticed.

"Don't get excited," Nerevin said. "You have a long way to go."

"Yes, *Master*."

She coated the word with thick playfulness, and Nerevin's eyes—Horace's eyes, lovely and brown and always so full of joy—flashed with anger. The expression was so out of place on her friend's face, it doused her own enthusiasm. There was too much at stake for Horace, and she had fallen into the patterns of her village, where they pushed and pulled at each other constantly.

The sort of banter that had made the air spark between her and Nene, the sizzling turning to love with time.

Keza's fingers curled into the loose soil beneath her hands, her claws sliding out as she resisted the surge of longing. She didn't want to be here, in this cursed marsh with this arrogant Fragment, training to master a fighting style that was both part of her tradition, and unheard of before. She wanted to be *home*, to argue and wrestle with Nene until Lena's soft voice interrupted them. She wanted to perch high in their house's rafters while Jael built massive structures of sticks with their nine little balls of chaos. She wanted to hear those happy screams when she returned home from hours scavenging through the mountain and the children rushed her.

It didn't matter, though. None of that mattered. She'd never make it home, wouldn't watch her kittens grow up, wouldn't sleep nestled between Nene, Lena, and Jael again. The best she could do was put it out of her mind and stop chasing the slightest hint of home. It wasn't like Nerevin could ever replace any of them, anyway.

"So, food," she said, dragging her thoughts firmly back to the present. "We didn't stock up before following the trail of Inae blooms."

"No matter," they said.

No matter? She couldn't complete their training if she starved—or if Horace did, for that matter. Keza opened her mouth to snap back and was rewarded by a stinging thwack before she could get a word out.

"Keep your sharp wits to yourself. The monastery was self-sufficient," they said. "Follow me."

Keza hissed but silenced any further retort— a true feat of willpower, on her empty stomach. Stiff and bruised, she fell into steps behind Nerevin, curious to see more of the abandoned monastery and her people's lost lives.

5

Fruits on the Vine

Keza had never seen so many Inae vines at the same time. They crawled across the sweeping hexagonal arches of the dilapidated green houses, curling up their broken remains to hang in long strands above the ground below, their blooms washing it in an entrancing blue light.

Underneath, fog coiled through rows of trellises overgrown by the bushes planted at their feet, which had grown so wild they'd crossed the alleyways and formed one massive tangle of vegetation. And on those, catching the light on darker blue skin, were fruits half the size of her palms clustered in small groups and tugging their vines downward with their weight.

"Those are … fruits from the Inae blooms?"

None of the blooms in Keza's stories climbed to such height or produced fruits, but she'd recognize her people's guides anywhere. The long leaves were the same, curling under the berries as if to scoop them up. She strode to the closest plant as certainty lodged itself in her chest, warm with wonder, and she lifted a cluster to examine them. Silence stretched in the overrun garden until she realized Nerevin hadn't replied.

They stared at her, studying her the way she studied the berries. "Of course they are," they said, enunciating each word very slowly before turning towards the overgrown mess. "They've not been cared for."

The tight wistfulness of their tone was almost as odd in Horace's voice as the sharp coldness had been. Keza had no idea how to deal with it, so she chose to ignore it.

"Can we eat them? Is that why we're here?"

Their face snapped back into anger. "Your people—our people—they have forgotten about the Inae berries?"

At their accusatory tone, Keza dropped the fruits and crossed her arms, tilting her chin up. "So what if we have? We're thriving. Unlike this awful marsh, there's plenty of other food to go around where I'm from."

Especially now. Nerevin didn't need to know how close they'd come to starving without the irrigation mechanisms left by the village's ancestors.

"You are an insolent, foolish brat. These are the fruits of our people, gifted to us by Inae, nurtured by generations of Inae monks whose names and dedication have been lost to time. They are not simply food, of which one can have plenty of."

Keza gritted her teeth. She'd heard the legends around the flowers, had always thought of them as sacred guides, and hadn't hesitated to follow the path when she'd spotted it. Of course these berries wouldn't be simple fruits, but she couldn't help her defensiveness. It wasn't her fault—or her village's fault—if they'd lost that knowledge. Not even the Elders had ever mentioned berries from the Inae blooms; no one must have eaten those in centuries at home.

But this asshole was from another time, weren't they? A time when Inae culture was more than a gathering of legends and a technique only a few ever mastered. A time when the abandoned tunnels in the mountains had been filled with people, when the glowing fungi painting mosaics on the walls had meant something. A time when masters of the *water dance* would have known to call it that and why. The loss of it all balled inside of her, a thick knot of anger she couldn't unfurl into anything kind.

"I've got bad news for you, *Master*. It's all gone. Your place is a ruin in a haunted marshland and no one has tended to these plants in centuries— no one even knows to find them or try. And at home? We see the vestiges around us and wonder at them, but we haven't got a clue about their real history, just that they were ours. The only Inae blooms left are flowers guiding us to the valley's village. Not a single berry to be had."

She grabbed one of the round berry again, snapping it off its branch before squishing it under palm and claw. The juice stained her russet fur and ran along her wrist to drop below.

"This is history now. Ghosts of a past no one cares about—like you."

She flung the berry at them and stalked off, ignoring the screams of her stomach. The loss gnawed even harder, and she couldn't stay here and get lectured about a tradition she had been forcibly ejected from. Was there a point to learning any of this when she could never bring it home?

The fruit hit Nerevin with a squish, splashing across their face. They had let it connect, as they'd wanted her to do with the rock.

They did not, however, let her leave. She'd almost reached the entrance archway when they moved, slamming both feet to the ground one at a time, a child throwing a tantrum in slow motion.

The earth answered, Nerevin's impact spreading in a grumbling wave, passing under her feet and to the arch—and there, the earth split with a crack, solid rock bursting through the muddier ground to bar the way. Keza stopped short and turned.

Nerevin had regained their initial posture, and berry juice clung to Horace's curls before dripping down. "You will sit, you will eat, and you will learn. It seems our illustrious battle technique will be the least of my teachings here."

A few minutes of shoving Inae berries into her belly left Keza feeling dazed and full. The fruits had a thick skin she could pierce with her claws, after which she squished the flesh out and into her mouth. Each of them tasted sweet with an underlying tartness that emerged the more she ate, and she was surprised by how few she needed to be satisfied. A blue stain remained on her fingers by the end and she fought the urge to hide them like a child.

Nerevin had stared at her as she ate each of

them, but with her last one gone, she no longer had a pretext to ignore them.

"They're good," she said. "Still feels sacrilegious to eat."

"This is their purpose," they said.

"Are they not guides?"

They turned up their nose, and Keza quickly squashed her rising aggressivity at their expression. Any talking back and she wouldn't get an answer, no matter how surface-level and condescending.

"In some stories," they admitted. "Metaphorical, of course."

"We literally tracked them to this place."

Nerevin didn't dignify this counterpoint with an answer, instead rising from their seated position and gesturing at her to follow.

"It is time to care for the garden before it chokes itself."

As far as Keza could tell, the garden had survived fine in the decades—if not centuries—it had been left to fend for itself. If anything, she'd call it thriving, in its own wild and chaotic way.

Nerevin, however, asserted that the original vines had been planted eight feet apart from one another in long rows, and that everything in between would hinder the vines' growth and needed to be weeded out. Nothing remained of the old order, but they seemed to know exactly which plants to keep, and which to pull. For someone who'd been so prompt to castigate her for a lack of respect, Nerevin was quick to discard the vegetation that had run wild. All to get the rest of them in neat little rows again.

It didn't sit well with Keza, who had always been one to run wild, and she tried to leave smaller plants intact in the hopes they'd escape notice. As soon as Nerevin verified her work, however, they caught them, scolded her, and dug them out of the earth with their hands.

"Why not use your powers?" she'd asked once, her frustration spilling over. "Is your control too imprecise?"

Nerevin only stared at her in silence for a *long* minute before walking off.

They gardened until the remainder of the

light vanished, its dull grey slipping away through the fog. Exhausted, battered, and emotionally drained, Keza had no desire to delay sleep.

"Is it safe here? Do you keep away other Fragments, too?"

Nerevin tilted their head to contemplate her question. "These Fragments … have you seen any of them here?"

She hadn't, which would be more reassuring if Nerevin sounded like they had any idea what "Fragments" meant. With the exception of the ones that composed the Earth Master, there hadn't been a single suspicious speck of gold since she and Horace had entered the monastery, though, so she decided that was good enough. Maybe the Earth Master's presence repulsed them like the Wagon did.

A pang of worry filled her as she thought of their curmudgeon transport and her friends left behind. If the roles had been reversed, she'd have hated being stuck, the Wagon unable to follow, half the group missing while another

Fragment storm could strike. But there was no way to contact them, and she couldn't abandon a possessed Horace. She'd have to learn, and quick, for which she needed to be rested.

When Nerevin leaned against a wall and closed their eyes, she found a crumbled pile of rocks, climbed to the top of it, and tried to snug her body between them and the wall. It was the most uncomfortable she had been in months, but she fell asleep instantly.

Nerevin dragged her back to the garden between each training session in the courtyard in an attempt to clear out the overgrown mess it had become, and "set the Inae vines back on the right path."

They began cycling between lessons. First the sparring, where she learned how to brace against impacts with her core strength instead of deflecting it, and how to channel all her muscles into powerful blows rather than sweeping in to strike from unexpected angles. It was difficult to wean off her instincts for fluidity and agility—to stop relying on the water dance—but Keza put every inch of focus into it and even in the heat of battle, she slowly learned to depend more on the sturdy and grounded postures that had allowed her to open the door. They were satisfying in their own way, sharp and distinct, forcing her to experience the fight less as a continuum, and more as a flurry of key moments.

Unfortunately for them, Keza was far more apt at mastering fighting techniques than farming ones. Any elder from her village could have told Nerevin that. They'd spent decades trying to instill Keza with a sense of the earth—to teach her to prune, or water, or whatever else—but she'd only ever gotten good at harvesting. When they'd finally given up on her, she'd been allowed more time to scout out for Fragments to scare off and had focused her efforts on foraging, so she'd still contribute to the food reserves.

Nerevin didn't give up. As they slowly cleared the garden, they instructed Keza about the life cycle of the plants, how to watch for bugs and treat the soil, as well as why the vines thrived even in thick fog or near darkness. It passed through her mind like water through a rocky soil, and she found herself wishing Horace was also listening in.

E would've loved to learn about all of this. It was easy to imagine em losing any sense of time as they pulled weeds and pruned vines, the damp fog clinging to eir curls and seeping into eir clothes. Sometimes Nerevin stopped moving, lost in their memories, and she could almost believe Horace was there with her, eir boundless enthusiasm easing her own reluctance. But the master's rigid posture was antithetical to everything Horace was, and the most minute twitch broke the illusion.

Her wistful hope for Horace only grew at the end of her fourth day of training, when she noticed a perfect hexagon of stone raised off the ground in front of the wall Nerevin chose to sleep against. When she asked about it, they waved it away. "It is for playing Birth of a Mountain."

Had she been truly on her own, she might not have cared. But she owed it to Horace, whose body had just been used to mention an unknown game with complete dismissiveness, to investigate.

"Playing?" she asked.

"A nonsense game; a mockery of the tales brought to life by the Inae techniques. I have enough to teach you without wasting our time on it."

She could almost hear herself telling Horace that games were for children, once upon a time. Keza hissed at Nerevin.

"Are games not part of our cultural heritage, then? Our traditions?" She examined the hexagon once again, taking in its age-old stains. "Where are those from? They look a little blue— I bet it's not a coincidence this is next to the Inae vineyard."

Their exasperated sigh was her first confirmation she'd won. "It is not. As your fingers can attest, Inae berries are quick to taint. We use them to create tints, but it has also led to the Birth of a Mountain challenge. Go find a dozen overripe fruits."

Nerevin waved her off, and Keza dashed for the overgrown vines, scooping up some of the large but flat stone bowls they'd unearthed earlier. She weaved through the plants to an area they'd not worked on yet, then tapped the hanging fruits with the tip of her claw as gently as possible. If the skin split regardless, she picked them up and placed them in the wide dish.

When she returned, Nerevin was waiting by the strange hexagon with their stone staff, their feet spread apart in the resting stance of the Inae earth cycle.

"Stand in the middle of the hexagon," they ordered, and as soon as she'd settled there, they added, "Now hold the dish above your head."

Keza had her first inkling of where this was going. The "bowl" had almost no lip at all, and the berries rolled around it with ease. She'd had to slow down as she followed the path back to Nerevin or risk spilling them out.

"You're about to make it impossible to keep them in there, yeah?" she asked.

"The mountain's strength is in stability. How well you do is measured by how clean the circle remains. One foot must always stay grounded."

Keza snorted. These people and their obsession with always having their feet touching the earth! "Bring it on."

Nerevin spun their staff then stomped the ground once, and the earth beneath Keza rumbled in warning. She locked eyes on them, letting the world fall away from her perception until there was nothing but her, the shifting weight of the large dish abovehead, and the Inae Master moving with Horace's body.

Then Nerevin erupted into action. They slammed their staff down and the stone cracked under Keza, a fault line between her two feet. Her claws dug into the ground as it lifted up, the chunk on her right rising and forcing her off balance. Her bowl tilted above her head, the Inae fruits rolling towards the edge. Keza extended an arm to balance them out before any could roll off, but she'd barely had any time to feel satisfied about it when Nerevin leaped from one position to another, and transformed the ground under her feet once again.

This time the crack ran under the arch of her left foot, and she slid it backward as the front half burst up, leaving claw marks in it before it flew past her face. The speed with which she'd moved tilted the dish back, and one of the fruits rolled off the low edge before she could right herself. It splashed at her feet, staining the stone, and she would have sworn she heard Nerevin chuckle despite the cacophony of grumbling, cracking earth.

Keza's jaw tightened. Nerevin migrated through various stances with ease, their shoulders squared as they stomped, shifted, slammed, and turned. This game would've brought childish glee to Horace, but eir lips barely curled now, held into a self-satisfied smirk by Nerevin. Her anger at eir possession, offered or not, crystallized. She wanted to win this, not for herself, but for em.

A low growl escaped her as she refocused on her body, the balance of the dish, and the whispers of the earth beneath of her feet. Her eyes locked onto Nerevin, but she barely saw them, one sense amongst many. The air smelled of foetid mud and stone dust, and it lay heavy on her fur.

When the circle under her feet cracked again, she let these senses guide her—the slight vibration under her claws, the tinge of dust raising, the shift in Nerevin's weight as they pounded their staff on the ground, and the hum of power that followed it. It registered faster than she could analyze, but her body knew how to react—and the longer it listened, the easier the pattern became.

Strange familiarity itched at the back of her brain while she moved with the quick rises of the stone circle, the Inae fruits rolling around her dish. She had seen Horace's body move in this fashion before, albeit with less certainty, eir transitions between positions bungled and powerless.

They had been at the monastery's entrance, staring at the carvings above it.

The hexagon door which had opened in chunks as she had pounded the ground one final time.

A ferocious grin spread across Keza's face. Armed with this knowledge, she began anticipating how the circle would break, what the next shift would be. It wasn't a perfect cycle—perhaps influenced by Nerevin's intent, or the current lay of the hexagon beneath her feet—but it had recognizable patterns, and that helped. Instead of scrambling to preserve her Inae fruits she moved with the changing ground, the dish barely tilting, and freed from the panicked rush to meet the shifts, her mind could listen better.

With every new slam of Nerevin's staff, Keza felt power shift through the earth as surely as she could track her own technique wrap through water. The water dance was an irresistible momentum that pulled current along, but this was a different relationship, in which keeping the body low and firm, its weight rooted in a squat, connected it to the earth and shared in its stability.

Keza wasn't sure she understood it, but she wanted to try. She'd grown quite good at managing very varied relationships—with everyone in the Wagon, of course, but also before that, with her partners. The four of them couldn't have been more different from one another. Wasn't that part of the fun?

She bid her time. There was a point in the cycle when the hexagon would partly reset itself, sections falling down to fuse with lower levels. She moved with the two sudden rises beforehand, staying ever so slightly ahead, then leaped up, breaking Nerevin's express rule to always keep one foot on the ground.

Not that it'd matter considering all the other rules she intended to shatter.

"Nerevin," she called, "it's your turn."

She slung the dish out with a spin, and one of the Inae fruits immediately rolled off the edge, smashing into Nerevin as their head snapped up. Keza spread her legs out, squatting down as she retrieved her staff from her back. When she hit the ground, she had fully assumed the first position above the door and slammed into the stone hexagon with all the force she could muster.

The stone vibrated under her claws, forming a thin and immaterial connection she felt in her core. Until then, stone had always been hard and dead to her, but this crystallized in her, rock-solid. It lasted a sliver of time, the instant gone as quickly as she had conjured it, and as she marvelled at it, the ground cracked under Nerevin, the lines creating a rough triangle barely bigger than a foot.

It lifted an inch, and the Earth Master lifted an eyebrow, seemingly unimpressed.

Stunned by her own accomplishment, Keza wasn't ready for their counterattack. They dropped the large dish to the ground, then stomped on its lid to flip it. The four fruits left in it flew up, and Nerevin caught each of them in turn—two on the up swing, two on their descent—and flung them at Keza.

The first smashed into her shoulder, painting it blue, but she managed to dodge the second, leaning out of the way. As the third arrive, she whacked her staff into it, aiming to return it to sender, but the fruit exploded on impact. A wild laugh escaped her as juice sprayed her and further stained her fur, and on impulse she stomped onto the ground, once more reaching for the earth. It rumbled, but the wall she'd been hoping for didn't burst upward to protect her, and instead the last Inae fruit smashed on her forehead. Her ears flicked reflexively, and she wiped most of it away, still laughing.

"You broke the rules," Nerevin declared with unflappable reproach.

"Broke the whole game, I think," Keza said. "Worth it to get some blue on you."

Nerevin snorted. "You're proud of yourself."

Their tone lacked its usual bite. Keza tried to contain the happy sweep of her tail. She was learning, and fast. Why wouldn't she be proud of herself?

"Enough of this nonsense," Nerevin said. "Let's hope the baths have survived the passage of time."

6

Heirs

Survive was an exaggeration.

The monastery's baths still existed, insofar as the room hadn't collapsed on itself, but the muddied water inside wouldn't clean anything. Keza might as well dive directly into the marsh; the result would be the same. It was, undoubtedly, a shitty, broken room that couldn't serve its initial purpose.

She couldn't tear her gaze away from it.

She *knew* this room—rather, she had been in one just like it. It'd also had a large hexagonal bath in the centre, stone benches on the three walls across from the entrance, archways rising from the corners to meet in the middle, with extruding patterns all over them that provided somewhere for Inae vines to cling and bloom, shedding their delicate blue light. It was all the same, except clear, warm water had filled hers, maintained through the mechanical wonder that had irrigated the village farms for centuries.

She had loved the baths. Few from the village ventured all the way out to them, allowing Keza to sink into the shallow water and unwind for hours—and not always alone. Lena had snuck away to them as frequently as Keza, and they'd made a game out of surprising each other that had spanned over a decade. Keza had lost count of how often they'd made love by or in the water, their intimacy slow and inexorable, the complete opposite of Keza's fiery trysts with Nene.

Small wonder that the baths had also been where Lena had forever changed Keza's life, one hot summer night when the caves and water had been a blessing. She had leaned against Keza, her white fur slick and wet, and simply declared in her eternally calm voice "Jael and I are expecting.

We think Nene and you should join us and care for the little ones."

To this day, Lena teased her for how long she'd stared ahead wordlessly. When someone in the village became pregnant, they built a child-rearing circle from their close relationships. It was tradition for the team of parents to include at least one other felnexi awaiting children, when possible, and anywhere between one and three without any offsprings on the way.

In theory, the circle was formed of potential role models. Responsible people. Keza—strong-headed and abrasive—hadn't thought she qualified, so all she'd eventually managed was a meek *"Me?"*

"Yes, you," Lena had repeated. "They'll need someone with a sense of community stronger than their obeisance. I want them to be loved beyond rules and conventions."

She had loved them more than anything—still loved them more anything—and they were horribly far away, irremediably torn from her.

Hot, acrid pain wormed its way up Keza's throat, lodging itself there as she fought the surge of grief and focused on the present. She couldn't return home, couldn't fix her exile.

"I can fix this," she said aloud, and Nerevin snorted.

Whatever. She didn't need *them* to believe in her. She was Keza Nesmit, a master of the water dance, and if she wanted to clean herself, she damn well would.

She let her decades-old mastery take over, the Inae technique of her village a second nature to her. She danced, her movements sweeping and fluid as she spun the staff around her, and the water responded. It rippled, dragged down by the mud, but its presence was a crystalline touch on her mind, pure and invigorating and familiar. She brought her entire body in a low swipe, then traced a half-circle up, reaching for the water, untangling it from the dirt, separating them as she had while fighting the trainees.

An elongated spurt of water burst up from the bath, so clear it reflected the Inae blooms' blue light all around. Keza grinned and spun on herself, swinging her staff in a diagonal arc perfectly aligned with the space between Nerevin and the water. It surged forth and splashed on them, drenching Horace's curls and washing away some of the blue juice.

"See?" she said. "Now you've been washed."

Nerevin wiped water from their cheek with a non-committal grunt, then stepped forward, to the edge of the bath. A thick dry coat of dirt filled the bottom; all that remained of the mud Keza had extracted.

"Perhaps we *can* fix this," they said, before falling into the low, square stance of the earth resolve. "Gather the water."

Keza hissed at the direct order, but obeyed it nonetheless. She had an inkling of what Nerevin had in mind, and she wanted to try.

As she slid into the patterns of the water dance again, Nerevin stomped the ground and moved through the sudden gestures of their own technique. The dirt at the bottom of the bath compressed, as if a great weight had slammed into it from above. Small particles rose in a cloud, but Nerevin sent them aside with a single sharp motion. Keza's concentration slipped as she watched them work, but instincts took over, her body flowing through the routine as she swept her staff left and right, scooping large swaths of water from the muddy marsh grounds and cradling it midair.

"Drop it," Nerevin said.

They had smoothed the inside of the bath, compressing it until not a single crack remained in the perfect hexagonal shape. Keza spun on herself and brought her staff in a long, powerful arc abovehead, sending the water into the tub with a great splash. When it came to rest, it was so clear they could see the bottom.

"Let's hop in and turn it blue, yeah?" Keza said, disrobing with enthusiasm before plunging into the water. When she noticed Nerevin's awkward hesitation, she added, "I have seen Horace in underwear before. E taught me to swim."

They removed the blue-stained shirt, and Keza couldn't help her relief that Nerevin still thought of this body as someone else's enough to have hesitated. After a lifetime of stories of Fragments forcefully possessing others until their body died, it was difficult to trust the Inae Master would relinquish control. She let herself relax in the bath, quietly wishing the water was warm enough to ease her bruised muscles.

"You could rebuild it."

Although they had adopted the same didactic, slightly condescending tone they always did, Keza caught the weight in their words, the seriousness of their hope. Her eyes snapped open, but she kept her gaze fixed on the vines clinging to the ceiling.

"Now there's an irony. Exiled from one clan only to inherit our long-lost traditions from another and rebuild their cradle."

She tried to imagine herself manipulating the surrounding earth to patch the monastery, or settling with some unknown trainees to care for its vineyard and baths. Her mind replaced the shapeless strangers with her family: Nene training in the courtyard, her posture a better earth resolve than Keza ever could; Lena patiently pruning the Inae vines to allow them to flourish, a full dish of fruits by her side; Jael wrestling their children into the bath waters as they screamed to escape.

The thought of her nine furballs pressed against her lungs and robbed her of breath. She missed their weight against her as they slept, missed their laughter as they ran after each other outside. She even missed the incessant fighting, the cleaning up after they spilled their meals, the restless nights caring for them as tiny babies. It was so easy to regret everything and wish she could be back there in one big huddle with them and Nene, Lena, and Jael.

Would they follow her into this cursed marsh, if she returned to fetch them? But no. It was preposterous. She couldn't ask them to abandon the lush valley of their village, and even if she dared ... how would she go back? They had almost reached Aliyah's forest, and she could no more ask the Wagon crew—her new family—to renounce their quest than she could ask her parent circle to desert their lives for her.

One day, perhaps. The Elders might not demand an immediate execution, if she returned with their lost traditions. After they had solved Aliyah's problem and journeyed to new cities, they could cross the ocean, travel to Keza's village, and risk it.

She needed to believe it was possible, that she might see her little ones and watch them grow again. Even if it hurt, even if the rational part of her knew better, she needed to nurse that hope the way Nerevin nurtured the gardens, tending to plants that'd be abandoned again as soon as Keza left, as if someone could restore it to its former glory.

"Your little broken-down monastery is the only parcel of this marsh that isn't haunted by deadly, roaming Fragments rolling over the landscape like a storm. No one wants to live here, least of all me."

She kept her voice steady, covering her ache with her own layer of mockery. Nerevin glared at her, stiff and cold once again.

"This was a sanctuary, built to honour all Inae had given us and to protect it from the Empire's trampling might. It was holy. But it seems one such as you has no grasp of what a higher calling means."

They stood up, water shedding all around them as they climbed out of the baths, leaving Keza seething. She had plenty to aspire to and her own life to live, and she wouldn't throw it all away because a long-dead master of her traditional arts had failed *their* calling.

Since she had felt the stone's echoes beneath her feet, Keza progressed much faster. She grasped the relationship between Nerevin's training exercises, the stable earth forms they were teaching her, and the impact on the dirt, stone, and mud around her. More than once, the ground rose beneath her claws, responding to her as she stomped.

Every time, she found herself glancing

towards Nerevin, who *must* have felt it. They only scoffed and pressed her harder.

This was their first training session since the Earth Master had left the bath with a huff. They'd lost most of the day to another of these freaky Fragment storms. It had passed overhead, screeching and howling but never diving into the monastery—proof that they were safe inside, if there ever was any. Keza hoped the same was true of the Wagon, Aliyah, and Rumi. She missed Rumi's never-ending ramblings, the Wagon's judgemental presence tracking her as she moved around, and Aliyah's quiet humour.

She'd been tempted to tell Nerevin about them—to explain all that had happened since the village—but she'd found them curled in the middle of the vines, lips moving in wordless whispers, eyes wide and unseeing.

"Nerevin?" she'd called, but the Fragments abovehead had exploded in a loud screech and buried her voice. Golden light had poured out of Horace's eyes, and she'd scrambled to eir side. "Horace?"

Neither of them had answered, but when she'd placed her hand on Horace's shoulder, Nerevin's memories had slammed into her. She had stood in the courtyard, gently instructing a young muscular elf as they tried to hold their ground against her assault, the bright sun pounding on them all. For an instant, the monastery had smelled of sweat, incense, and fresh grass rather than rot and stagnant water. Keza had pulled back with a gasp, and stood watch over her friend as the storm passed.

Nerevin hadn't made mention of it. As soon as they had recovered from the storm, they had stomped to the courtyard, barking for Keza to follow.

They had only become more aggressive since. Their snark had moved from "stop dodging and start taking, water dancer" when she learned to block and parry, to "even a child could do better" as she mastered the postures, and now that she could get the earth rumbling for her, all they had to say was "how did one such as you ever mastered *any* of the Inae arts?"

Keza had had enough. Horace and her had been gone for too long already. She wasn't one of Nerevin's old students they could berate endlessly, and she wouldn't learn much more from them at this rate. She leapt back from their ongoing fight and set the butt of her staff on the ground, putting a clear end to it.

"Enlighten me, Master. What in all the cursed stars is wrong with you? Is abusing the trainees also part of the earth resolve?"

Deep anger flashed through their eyes, and the snarl curling their lips was a frightening thing on Horace's normally soft face. "I did not need to 'abuse' our trainees. They had a sense of discipline and duty you utterly lack."

Ah yes, her poor discipline. The bane of every Elder who'd tried to instruct her. The one Nerevin supposedly shared with her, and the one she'd done her best to cull for Horace's sake, submitting herself to their berating. That couldn't be the problem; they needed a pretense.

"Sounds to me like you'd already broken them," she spat back. "Is that the way of the stable earth? Get good little soldiers mindlessly ready to do anything for you? 'Cause we might as well stop now."

Nerevin sprang on her, their stone staff coming down in a single, powerful arc. She slipped out of the way at the last moment, but the ground under her feet cracked and surged up as the staff impacted, sending her stumbling. In that fraction of second of imbalance, Nerevin punched through her defenses with a powerful strike, cracking down on her hip. Pain flared through her body and she hit the ground, sinking into the softer mud.

"Run your tongue again and I'll smash every teeth out of your mouth." They towered over her, glaring down, and by the stars, Horace had never looked so terrifying, nor been so *infuriating*—and e could be the latter, in eir own way. "You don't know the sacrifices you disparage."

"Do *you*?" She pushed herself back up, testing out the strain on her hip as she brought her staff to bear again. "My discipline is fine, I can almost move earth as you do, so what's your real problem?"

Nerevin began circling her, their staff spinning in slow circles. "I'm afraid you're not the student I've been waiting for. How can I dishonour my students' sacrifice with one as self-centered as you? An exile with no heir! Our traditions would die with you."

Exile. Self-centered. Was that was they thought? All the anger coiling in her spilled out in a long, bitter laugh—because they were right about that much: she was bitter. She'd risked everything to keep her people fed and they'd rewarded her for it by casting her out. And now this bastard thought they had any room to judge her over it.

"Fuck you," she spat.

They sighed, the sound so deep and long it seemed to emerge from the deepest caverns. "It is as I thought. I cannot let Inae's earth resolve die with you. Your friend will have to forgive me, but until I find a proper replacement, I will need keep eir body."

Keza's fur puffed in response, fury tightening every hair on her body. This asshole. Was she always going to be unworthy? She had kept such a tight hold on her temper, tried to show her eagerness to learn, and all they'd wanted was an excuse to steal Horace's body. Well, she wouldn't let it happen, wouldn't let her own failings, perceived or otherwise, steal the rest of Horace's life away from em.

She growled and sank into herself—into decades of training much older than this bullshit, an attunement to her body and form unlike any other, a sense of movement and speed and precision, of powerful shapelessness.

Then she rushed Nerevin.

Keza's assault crashed against their mountainous defense in a flurry of blows that chipped without provoking real harm, coming and going in intensity like a wave's ebb and flow. Water pooled at her feet as she danced, twirling around her ankles as if to dance alongside her before splashing back down.

Over and over, she darted back in, spinning

and twirling, her eyes tracking Nerevin's defenses, the stillness and sudden movements, the steadiness of their posture. She'd crack it, she had to, if she just kept attacking, a hundred swings and stabs, a hundred sidesteps and jumps—there! A weak point, the tiniest of unbalance, one heel out of line. Almost nothing, but Keza pressed her advantage, and she focused on the Earth Master's left side until the barrage forced a step back, creating an opening.

Keza plunged in and smashed the butt of her staff in Horace's nose. It cracked with an explosion of blood and Nerevin staggered back. They wiped it with their hand, then flicked the blood to the ground with a laugh.

"Is that your plan? Beat your friend's body bloody? You cannot make me leave." They prodded at the nose, eyebrows shooting up. "It has been a long time since I've experienced physical pain to this extent. It is so paltry—meaningless, compared to what I have endured."

Keza's lungs burned from the exertion of her frantic assault, and the heaviness of her limbs was only made worse by the despair coiling into her. Abandoning Horace was not an option. If only Aliyah was there; she could probably expulse Nerevin.

"What's *your* plan?" she snarled. "That Fragment storm knocked you right out. You'd never escape this marsh, and no one would find you in here."

"I *must* try. The Inae berries will nourish my body and guide my path, and I will find one worthy of our teachings."

One who wasn't her. The rejection burned harder than she wanted to admit. She'd *wanted* to learn and had tried her best, yet Nerevin had still found fault in her. How was this any different than the Elders' exile? Somehow, she was never good enough for her people.

The only ones who hadn't rejected her lived in a pompous sentient Wagon—one she'd named herself after, now—and she refused to let Nerevin steal one of them.

"I can't let you." She brought her staff about in a slow twirl and paced until she stood between them and the main exit. "You'll find I am more than your match when I'm not trying to imitate your style."

Nerevin burst out laughing, a jagged and cruel sound that distorted Horace's hearty laughter. "For a time, maybe, but can you keep it up? How does your hip fare, Keza Nesmit? Your arms? Your lungs? Do they not still burn from your pointless dance?"

She hissed, because that was better than admitting they were right. All that training *she* had given Horace over the course of the last months had made em more endurant, and Nerevin knew how to exploit that to its maximum. If she fought him without a strategy, she'd lose.

"I thought so."

They spread their feet apart again, and their grip slid on the staff. Battle ready. She gritted her teeth.

"Your shoulder was badly wounded, too," she retorted, hoping to gain time while her mind ran through everything she knew about the situation.

"This isn't even the body you learned to fight in, and you're not alone in there." She had to hope that made a difference. Keza leaned back, arms crossed with a bravado she didn't feel. "You really think Horace will let you kick my ass?"

"E understands self-sacrifice better than you ever could."

E did. E obviously did, because she would never have given her body to this shithead. But that hadn't been what Horace had done either. E'd negotiated something temporary, trusting that e'd return eventually, and Nerevin was abusing that trust.

"Is that what happened to your trainees? They offered one Inae fruit and you ate the whole cluster and called it a sacrifice?"

Nerevin's head flinched as if slapped. Keza's heart pounded, details of their first encounter in this courtyard returning. These Fragments had been their apprentices, hadn't they? And they'd formed Nerevin's core.

"They died to preserve our traditions and our ways," they bit off.

"Like Horace is supposed to." She had them on the defensive now—emotionally, if nothing else. "No wonder you got so pissy. You *have* to think of them as willing sacrifices, happy to do their duty for the cause, otherwise what does that make you?"

She could almost pity them, the sole survivor of a tradition everyone else had died for, left with nothing but an empty monastery and fragmented pieces of their memory to fill it with. She might have, if they hadn't declared themself the new owner of her friend's body.

"I will hear no more of this," Nerevin declared with dangerous finality.

And that was all the time she got to think strategy. She wished she had Aliyah's quick mind and viciousness for it, but Keza's best skills had always been in breaking the rules and bringing the unexpected to the table. Perhaps she could do the same here, and make her own rules.

Nerevin rushed her with a overhead blow, forcing her to leap to the side. She landed with her feet spread out—earth style—and when they pressed on with a side swipe she caught it with the full strength of her body. Surprise flashed through their expression at the switch, and she taunted the Earth Master with an inquisitive *mreow*?

Nerevin doubled down on their offensive with a derisive *tsk*, forcing Keza to switch without pause between water dance and earth resolve as she dodged, deflected, and parried. The fluidity of her change clearly unnerved them, but even so, she was losing ground. Every new strike forced her deeper into the defensive, giving Nerevin more space to maneuver. When they found time to slam the butt of their staff to the ground and the earth split between her feet, she knew she needed to change the pace of this fight, and quick.

She leaped away to buy herself a handful of seconds. Nerevin stomped the ground, sending chunks of stone flying her way, and for a brief moment deadly golden light leaked from their eyes.

It was the inspiration Keza needed. She might

not have Aliyah to appease Nerevin, but they remained a collection of hostile Fragments inhabiting her friend's body, and for as long as she'd known them, the Inae techniques had *always* served as a defence against Fragments.

Keza had no time to figure out the details of *how*, as Nerevin rushed right back into the fight. She paced herself, waiting for another opportunity to break away, and when Nerevin swung in a wide horizontal arc, she dropped flat to the ground and smacked their feet with her staff. It barely made them flinch, but that split second let her get a knee and leg under her and surge forward, bodyslamming into them. They fell into the mud together, but she leaped back to her feet with a quick roll.

It wouldn't take long for Nerevin to spring back into the fight, but a handful of seconds was all she needed to test a theory. As an Inae Master, she had never needed to touch the Fragments to keep them at bay.

She spun her staff through the familiar sequence: a low twirl followed by sweeping up with a somersault, then spinning abovehead as she herself turned towards Nerevin to finish the routine. Water drops leeched from the mud under her feet, climbing towards the staff, power building with every step. Her grip tight on the staff, Keza brought it down in a wide, diagonal arc.

The gathered power slid down her weapon, bringing with it a wave of dirty water. Her heart leaped to her throat as it crashed against Nerevin, staggering them. Gold flared again through Horace's eyes, leaking around em before vanishing, leaving only an annoyed expression as Nerevin wiped off water and shook their blonde curls.

"Was that supposed to impress?" they asked.

A hint of confusion lay buried under their snark. Did they not understand what she'd attempted? But of course, Nerevin had never had to defend their people from Fragments. They would have no idea the Inae techniques were passed down as ways to disorient and repulse Fragments, that the protection thus given was tied to the sanctity of them for Keza and her village.

Which would be way more exciting if it had *worked*. The Fragments forming Nerevin had tied themselves too deeply into Horace. She needed to unmoor them first, somehow, to break that accursed earth stability.

Water wouldn't be enough. With time, it might erode Nerevin's strength enough for her to push them out, but she didn't *have* time. Neither did she have the mastery to beat Nerevin at their own game.

"Give up."

Nerevin's smarmy tone swept away the strands of despair. Her lungs burned, her hip screamed with pain, and her arms felt heavy from exertion, but she grinned at them.

"Sorry, not in my vocabulary."

She dove back into the fight, her mind scouring all she knew about the Inae techniques as her staff met with Nerevin's, wood against stone. The rythmic *thwacks* told their own story: short bursts of action as each fighter tried to pierce the other's defences, then a slower pause as they drifted apart, recovering and reevaluating. Every battle had its tale.

The thought collided with others—how the Inae techniques told the story of water and earth, how obsessed with heroes and prophecies the Archivists were, how Fragments so forcefully demanded that Aliyah listen to their stories. How much power crackled in each of these things.

This is what she needed. A new story, one that would rip Nerevin out of Horace's body. Her mind latched onto the tales of disaster Aliyah had shared from the kraken's Fragments as they crossed the ocean, and she modelled her assaults after them.

First came waves after waves crashing into a town, each one bigger than the other—her strikes came in bundles of quick successive hits, numbers increasing with each new assault, water gathering around her.

The ocean's floor followed, mud and stones and bones rising with the tide, carried into the town by its sheer force—and she leaped, spinning to block a hit before widening her grip to bring her entire staff down on Nerevin, catching them in the chest.

The disaster left thick walls of mud behind, burying everything—Keza landed, legs on each side of their prone form, stance wide, and the ground exploded at her feet, two waves reaching for one another to cover them.

Survivors walked through the wreckage under the rain, grief strangling them as they wrestled with memories of homes now lost—she spun the staff above Nerevin then swept it down, and the water curled into a single strand and plunged in Nerevin's throat, choking them.

In the end, friends and families huddled, hugging and crying in each other arms, there even when all else had been erased, grounding one another—she squared her body and squatted down, every inch braced by the power gathering inside her, a force unlike anything she'd ever felt, building and building within her battered muscles in a slow, tremendous grind.

Keza slammed her palm into Horace's chest, releasing everything she had.

Golden water spat out of eir mouth, swirling midair until it reformed into a small person built out of eight Fragments. Horace rolled over, coughing and spitting, a strand of gold still tied to em. With a screech like grinding metal, Nerevin plunged back, but she slammed the butt of her staff into the link before it could reach Horace. It cracked, falling into dust.

Panting, her hip a burning bulge of pain, her head dizzy from the power that had coursed through her, Keza glared at the Fragments.

"Give up," she said, echoing their ultimatum. "E's not yours."

"Keza?" Horace's voice, ragged and weak but so beautifully full of innocent love. "What?"

7

Unmired

Cheers rose from the nearby courtyard, disrupting Nerevin's concentration. The trainees were playing again, using Inae's sacred gifts for amusement.

Once, they would have been with them. As an apprentice, they'd loved to be the Creator, leaping and stomping their way through the Birth of a Mountain cycle, putting their peers off balance with the strength and stability of their routine. Watching others perform had also taught them; they were all recounting the same story, but its shape varied with the teller.

But there was no more time for games. It had been decades since Inae had sent them into hiding, splitting her four traditions and swearing them to secrecy, and the threat she had foreseen was coalescing. The prophesized Cataclysm was coming, and they did not trust the Empire's solution. The monastery needed to be prepared; they had to endure.

"Master. Is today the day?"

Young Ghethin stood in front of them, staff at the ready, their shock of black hair now down at their shoulders, parting only for their pointed ears. They must have heard the cheer, too, and known it would herald the beginning of their next training. The others would follow soon, strolling in with a carefreeness Nerevin hadn't felt in ages.

"It is." They waited for the seven missing apprentices to file in and line up before continuing. "Today, I will teach you all to use the mountain's strength as an impenetrable defence—not as an individual, but as a group. Today, you will learn to link your resolve and build the Wall."

One by one, their bodies failing, they went through the motions, adopting the Wall posture, building a

mountain around the Master. One by one, they crumpled, golden light pulled out of them until their body collapsed and only broken shards remained. Ghethin was the last to fall. Nerevin watched, incapable of moving, their own stance maintained to perfection despite the burning, all-encompassing pain. They couldn't afford to twitch—they were the summit, the joining point of all mountain sides, the core of their defence and the last line of it.

Nerevin watched their trainees die to protect them. To protect their traditions and all this monastery represented. All eight fell, leaving crumbling walls behind, but they held on, minutes of agony turning into hours, every ounce of their endurance tested to the extreme.

But the pull was relentless, overwhelming. Alone in the courtyard, their vision flagged, their knees buckled, and something jerked through their throat, all sharp edges and endless, searing pain.

Horace woke to jagged pain in eir throat and the most agonizing coughing fit of eir existence. E tasted of blood and iron, and when e blinked out eir tears, eir vision focused on Keza's russet fur.

"Keza?" e mumbled, and the sound of eir own voice helped em find eir bearings. The courtyard. They were in the monastery's courtyard and eir entire body throbbed from exertion. Above, Nerevin's Fragments floated, detached from em. "What?"

"Don't worry," Keza said with a growl. "I got you."

Horace pushed emself up with eir elbow, sliding out from under Keza. Mud covered eir legs for some reason. What had happened here? Why did she sound so tense? Was this the same day? The grey skies were no help there.

"Got me?" She had her eyes on the Fragments, her fur standing on end, and looked ready to dive into battle. "But they were supposed to teach you."

She snorted. "Yeah, well, that didn't pan out."

Nerevin had been so adamant about it, so eager. Maybe Horace was still confused, eir mind too full from memories not eir own and the nightmare they'd led to. "What happened?"

Keza hissed. "They're an asshole and tried to steal your body."

Nerevin's screeched in answer, their words jagged with anger, resonating in eir head. *"She was not a worthy student."*

"Not worthy?" e repeated. "But you *wanted* to teach her. You saw her fight and it was all you could think about."

"And I kicked their ass with their own technique. By the stars, I blended my style and theirs into a whole new story just to smash them out of you, and somehow I'm still not worthy?" Her tail twitched, but despite the rage bubbling in her voice, Horace thought she mostly looked *exhausted*. She was leaning on her staff, her shoulders sagged. "It has nothing to do with worthiness, Horace. They learned I'd been exiled, and suddenly I was a selfish piece of shit and they wanted another student."

That didn't even make any sense. Horace's gaze went between the two of them, and e slowly pushed emself on wobbly feet. "Keza," e said, "you got yourself exiled to save Rumi, and because *I* followed you. And that happened because your people were starving and you made us help. That's the reverse of selfishness."

She huffed and clung to her staff tighter, and suddenly e understood.

"You didn't tell them any of that, did you?" e asked.

"I don't owe them an explanation after they treated me like shit. And why would they believe it anyway?"

Horace turned slowly towards the Fragments, hovering nearby with the arms sagged down, looking strangely defeated themself.

"*It matters not,*" they said. "*She has no one to pass the knowledge to. I cannot let it die here. You saw what we sacrificed to preserve what little is left of me.*"

Welp. At least they believed Keza? When Horace had given up eir body, e hadn't expected to return to it and find those two fighting like angry children. E'd hoped Keza would have learned new tricks and maybe filled some of the holes created by her exile. It sounded like they'd instead poked at each other's wounds until they were so raw they couldn't think through the pain, and Horace's nose had paid for it. It throbbed endlessly, and when e pressed a hand to it, eir fingers came back bloody.

At least Horace had a lot of experience talking down fighting children. Eir prolonged stay in Clan Nissa had turned em into every child's older, wiser sibling and a de facto mediator for their quarrels. E first ambled towards Nerevin, eir hair rising as e came so close to the Fragments that one wrong spin would cut em.

"I did, and I *understand* what you've been through and those you wish to honour. I'll remember the vineyard, the times of meditative silence, the scrappy youth finding their balance here. I promise." E offered a hand, palm up, for Nerevin to rest onto. "We'll unearth someone to pass your teachings to. Keza has her whole life before her, and if her village is too foolish to hear her, then it'll be somewhere else. You've done your duty."

Surprise flitted through the Fragments in a quick twirl, then one of the eight came to rest on Horace's palm, flat against eir skin. It left a buzzing sensation. The rest of the Fragments slid downward, their spin slower.

"Too much has been lost already. I must find someone. I simply must."

The metallic screech slipped into their voice once more and fear pinched Horace's heart as agitation spun their Fragments. It took all eir control not to snatch eir palm back. E didn't want to be possessed again. The world still felt shaky and distant from Nerevin's time in eir body, and e wasn't sure Keza could free em twice.

"The secret to Inae's earth resolve is in good hands with Keza," e said, "but we know someone for the rest of your traditions, too. For everything I didn't see. She can listen, commemorate, repeat. She can grant you peace. She has done so for countless Fragments before."

"Fragments," they repeated, and though

they'd not phrased it as a question, Horace would have sworn they didn't understand. When e turned to Keza, she shrugged.

"I don't think Nerevin grasps what they are." Her tail swept the muddy ground, the only outward sign of her own agitation. "The Wagon hadn't, not at first, no?"

"Then they should meet the rest of the crew!" Horace turned to the Earth Master's floating Fragments with a grin and moved eir hand from under one of them, to above it, as if e'd wanted to grab theirs. "Come with us."

Nerevin slunk back. "*Away from the monastery?*"

Their voice pierced the foggy air with both the screech of metal and utter contempt. Horace recoiled from them, but Keza remained unimpressed. She stepped between them, staff at the ready but strangely relaxed.

"That was your exact plan seconds ago. I know you're a stubborn prick, but maybe you owe it to Horace to give it a shot after you tried it with eir stolen body."

Her retort was met by silence. Better than the angry metal scraping noises, certainly, and it granted Horace a moment to fight the shock of heat coursing through em at the reminder of Nerevin's betrayal.

"Very well, Horace ve'Elzear," the Earth Master eventually said. *"I will follow, and trust that our sacred traditions will be reignited in time. Even if it must be through Keza."*

"You don't have to sound so reluctant about it," Keza retorted. She received a great, metallic *harrumphed* in response, one of the strangest noises Horace had ever heard, and her tail twitched. "Let's move. I'd rather we reach the Wagon before it gets dark, and I think we should gather Inae fruits for our supplies first."

She stalked out of the courtyard with haste, and Horace knew better than to hurry after her. E recognized the tension in her shoulders and the quick escape. She wanted to be left alone, scouting ahead where she could deal with her emotions in private. E bought her time by moving eir arms, legs, neck, and wrists one by one, as if testing for bruises and other wounds. After a moment, Nerevin hovered closer.

"I also owe you an apology," they said. *"You entrusted your body to me, and I dishonoured our arrangement."*

"I don't mind. I mean—I do, but it's all right. It's…" Horace stopped blabbering. E still felt like a jumbled, disconnected mess of emotions. "I wish you hadn't, but I'm not angry."

"Nevertheless, I would like to make amends while it is possible."

"Then apologize to Keza, too. She's prickly but she cares, you know. These are her traditions, not mine, and she's already sacrificed everything to keep her village alive."

The shards hissed, then the two forming Nerevin's shoulders sank downward and they drifted side-to-side. Sulking, Horace guessed. They knew e was right, whether they wanted to admit to it or not.

"Let's catch up to her," e said. E had seen the gorgeous vineyards in Nerevin's memory and was eager to explore them emself—or whatever was left of them, at any rate. "It's been a long day, but I'll be happy to be with the Wagon again. The two of you would get along. Or fight endlessly, perhaps."

"*I have had my fill of battles,*" Nerevin declared before drifting after Keza.

Silence pressed on Horace's shoulders as they trekked back towards the Wagon, heavier than the fog. Keza stayed ahead, guiding them from one Inae bloom to the next and never allowing Horace and Nerevin to catch up. Her extended need for privacy worried Horace, and e wished e had memories of what had happened while Nerevin controlled em to understand.

Neither of the involved parties wanted to share with em, though. The pair of them had avoided each other in the vineyard, plucking the Inae fruits in stubborn, sullen silence. Keza and Horace had left without equipment, and with the monastery in ruins, they'd had to be creative for transportation. They'd filled some of the large and shallow dishes available with the fruits, before setting another on top and tying them together with vines, two bowls creating a temporary container. One of those dug into Horace's back as e walked through the marsh, the pain grounding em further back into eir body. It was starting to feel normal again.

The Wagon's cyanwood emerged through the fog, a welcome sight that made Horace forget all about eir sullen companions, the bruises e had inherited, and the dangers of the marsh's roads. E rushed forth with a squeal, and not even the thick layers of mud still burying the Wagon's legs could dampen eir excitement.

Eir right foot sank into hidden waters and the alarming splash was eir only warning before eir still-stiff muscles locked in protest at the sudden change. Horace barely managed to snap eir mouth shut as e fell face first into the water, and the stagnant pool filled eir nostrils.

Keza pulled em out, chuckling as e sputtered and flailed, more from surprise than anything else. A jittery metallic sound joined her. Was Nerevin also laughing at em? E shook the muddy water from eir curls and turned towards the tinkling Fragments.

"You don't get to laugh if you don't even have to worry about where you set your feet down."

"*Convenient that I have no feet,*" they said, and although their Fragment-voice still held that broken-scraps quality, it had softened. Perhaps the long silence, stifling as e'd found it, had been good for them.

"Horace?"

Aliyah's voice pierced through the fog, and once e blinked the water out of eir eyes, e spotted her on top of the Wagon, leaning so far forward she risked falling.

"Aliyah!" e called back.

When e set off running again, e slowed eir pace enough to pick eir path, and soon e'd reached the muddy space where the Wagon had gotten bogged down. Aliyah vanished from the top to reappear a second later at the door, tattered cape flying behind her as she leaped into eir arms. E caught her, stunned by the unusual show of affection, and spun her around—almost out of habit, from all the kids e'd spun through the years. When e finally set her down again, she stepped back and cleared her throat as if to reclaim her dignity.

"Where *were* you?"

"Oh, I can't wait to tell you everything! Well, not everything, I wasn't exactly there for all of it, so to speak, but I'm sure Keza can fill in the holes. She was."

"Horace, you've been gone for five days. You left without a word. We were worried sick, then another Fragment storm buried us in deeper."

Five days? *Five days?* Panic swept through Horace. All this time e thought e'd woken up the same day e'd let Nerevin take over! Neither them nor Keza had rectified any of this, and sure, it'd felt like they'd been extremely busy in such a short period, but e'd never stopped to reflect on what that could mean.

"I-I'm sorry," e said, "I didn't … realize?"

An answer which only worried Aliyah

further, judging by the wrinkle across her forehead.

"It's my fault," Keza said.

"Of course it's your fault," Rumi chided from the Wagon's doorway, where he stood with his arms crossed. "We know Horace wouldn't have run off alone like that. E'd have wanted us all to see whatever cool thing had just caught eir eyes. Though it looks like e dragged it back to show it to us."

"I missed you too, shortscales. Give me more shit and I'm leaving your Wagon stuck in all this mud. I can move it all now, you know."

A long wooden creak of protest interrupted whatever answer Rumi had planned, and the Wagon's grating voice interjected. "I would appreciate not being punished for Master Rumi's peculiar welcome, especially when your absence rendered void his ability to focus on any engineered solution."

Keza grinned as Rumi hurriedly shushed at the Wagon, as if he had any power to stop it from revealing his secrets.

"I'd have come back, but then this asshole possessed Horace and I didn't dare leave em alone."

Nerevin had remained immobile through the reunion, the eight Fragments drifting close to one another. Now they spun quickly on themselves once, an angry twirl that was soon followed by a bristling correction. *"Permission was granted."*

"Permission was extracted," Keza snapped.

Aliyah turned to Horace. E shrugged. "I said yes."

Keza offered a clipped version of events. Horace had expected unyielding harshness towards Nerevin, but although her words were sharp, her tone brimmed with melancholy. She skimmed over the worst of their fight, without explaining why Nerevin had stopped teaching her at all, and everyone let it slide. When she was finished, the group's attention focused to Aliyah.

"Can you help them?" Horace asked.

A line of tension tightened in her shoulders. She hadn't touched a Fragment since they'd escaped Sioreze, and e wondered if she'd prefer not to ever again. They'd avoided discussing it at length, and now e didn't have a chance to ask ahead of time.

After a moment of silence, she sighed. "Whenever you are ready."

"I have a final request," they answered.

Keza whipped about, her tail flicking through the air with obvious displeasure. The two Fragments at Nerevin's shoulders floated up at her reaction, a defiant gesture reminiscent of raised eyebrows.

"Master Keza Nesmit intends to remove the mud from your... Wagon." Nerevin paused there, and Horace wondered how they perceived the Wagon. "I'd like to witness it."

"*Ah.* A final test, huh? Were you too close when I last pulled this off?" Keza gave her staff a lazy spin, then sprinted to the Wagon and jumped onto its top platform in one graceful leap. Once there, she turned around and pointed her weapon at Nerevin. "Peel whatever eyes you got in there. This'll be unlike anything you've ever done."

Rumi scampered away from the Wagon to stand with the rest of them as Keza fell into a ready position. Horace's gaze locked on her. E'd missed every bit of training and triumph, eir own mind lost in Nerevin's memories, and e was eager to see firsthand what she had learned. She was always so beautiful to watch.

Although the Wagon's roof was over a metre above from the mud she needed to move, she started spinning her staff overhead, the motion slow and deliberate, then accelerating. She dipped her upper body at regular intervals, swinging the staff along, and with every new cycle, the mud inched up, dislodging from the ground. It formed a strange ring around the Wagon, clinging to it as if it'd wanted to float but couldn't fully detach itself from the earth.

Then Keza completely changed her rhythm. She jumped up, bringing her staff overhead, and landed with her feet spread out, body and staff hitting the deck with one powerful *thump*.

The ring of mud stuttered up, snapping from the ground, and Keza grinned as she swept back to her original twirling, dancing moves, to gather another circle of mud. Always the same routine: fluid spins to grasp the water in the ground, then a leap and a brutal landing to dislodge everything from below. She repeated the process over and over, merging the rings in a crown above the Wagon, freeing its legs one inch at a time.

Power thrummed in the air, and Horace had no doubt that if she stopped moving—if she let it go—it would either explode outward or collapse back down. Hopefully back down, to the ground, but also hopefully neither of those, really!

Keza's expression curved into a playful smirk as she gathered mud, then she flicked a handful at Rumi, triggering offended cries from him. Horace had started laughing when eir own splash of mud hit em, and as e wiped it away, e saw Aliyah duck under her projectile. The entire Wagon crew was in various states of recovery when Keza sped her whirlwind spin then leaped down, bringing her staff down in an overhead sweep and sending the mass of sludge crashing on Nerevin's Fragments. They didn't flinch as it slammed into them. After a second, Keza dispatched it with a casual swipe.

The mud flew off and splashed into the marsh, settling into puddles and on the lilac-grey reeds, creating a clear path forward. The buzzing pressure of power in the air released, leaving behind a quiet silence. Pure awe filled Horace's chest and burst out into a cheer. E rushed to Keza and grabbed her shoulders.

"That was incredible! I can't believe I missed you doing that the first time around." Keza's ear flicked, and combined with the slight tilt of her head, Horace knew she was suppressing a more overt pride. E had no qualms heaping more praise onto her, though. "Between water and earth, you'll be unstoppable! A real Inae Master!"

Her ears drooped. "Don't push it. There's a lot I don't understand still."

"Indeed." Nerevin's voice cut through eir cheering with its metallic ting, "But you have proven you can learn in your own time if you try."

The upper half of the Fragments leaned forward, mimicking a bow. Keza stared back, tension tightening in her shoulders as she reciprocated.

"I will. Plenty of time to kill on this trip, and no shortage of dirt to fling about." Her claws tapped along her staff, then she sighed. "Thank you for the mentoring. I... We have but the barest of understanding of where our traditions came from, of what the Inae techniques even *are*."

"It is neither of our faults that this knowledge has been lost. I do not believe what happened to my monastery was coincidence. What matters now is that it survives." They turned to Aliyah. "I'm ready. Whatever it is you do."

"A question we would all like an answer to." Aliyah's voice shifted, growing deeper and gaining a strange, twisting echo. Bark covered her hands, her fingers elongated as they transformed into twigs. "I listen, I learn. Others like you have found peace in it."

Nerevin's Fragments spun slowly, humming

in quiet acknowledgement. "Perhaps it is time for me to rest, then."

Aliyah needed no other permission. She lifted her twig fingers and plunged them through the golden hue that connected the shards. Nerevin's head Fragment tilted upward, and with a final sigh, all eight of the Earth Master's parts turned into shimmering dust. It floated midair, glittering in the marsh's fog, a startling splash of colour in the grey landscape.

No matter how often Horace witnessed the phenomenon, it remained breathtaking. E hovered closer, ready to catch Aliyah as the golden dust drifted to her bark skin, clung to it, then sank into her. She swayed and squeezed her eyes shut, so e wrapped eir arms around her and let her lean into eir chest. Was she seeing the same memories e had? Or would she learn more, grasp it more deeply than either e or Keza could? There was still so much to understand—about Nerevin's life and the world before the Fragments, about Aliyah's powers, about Nerezia as it was now, haunted and broken.

But they were almost there.

At the centre of this marsh was the forest of Aliyah's dreams, the one they had set out to find all those months ago in Trenaze. Whatever they discovered in it, they would at least have answers.

8

To the Forest's Edge

When Horace emerged on the Wagon's roof early on the first morning after their return, e found Keza with her hands wrapped around her staff, her legs spread widely in one of the earth technique's postures, her face pinched with focus. She leaped from one position to the next, a foot forward as the weapon came down into a strike, then a third—sideways, this time—and finally looped back. The sequence was a burst of activity followed by tense immobility, and e watched wordlessly, marvelling at how different it was from the constant churning of her water dance.

Morning sessions had been their time

together, Keza teaching em what she could about battle, criticizing eir technique and acknowledging eir progress in equal parts. Compared to her, e was still a rookie, but e'd grown into a decent fighter over the months. She'd only needed a handful of days to grasp this new style, though. Did she learn exponentially fast? Or had Nerevin's training been far more gruelling? The Earth Master had been pressed for time and had been driven by centuries of unfulfilled duty.

Horace got so lost in eir thoughts, e didn't notice Keza had finished her routine until she prodded at em with the butt of her staff. The poke was gentle, but it pushed at bruises acquired by Nerevin, and Horace hissed at the unexpected pain.

"That's a new one," e mumbled, rubbing the spot on eir arm. "I wonder how long I'll keep finding those."

Keza laughed, and the sudden bark-like sound filled eir chest with warmth. She'd been playful throughout the rest of yesterday's evening, trading banter with the Wagon and Rumi while Aliyah recovered, eyes closed, but there'd been a sharpness to her voice that had never left.

It was gone now, and when she helped Horace up, she pulled em into a surprise hug, holding em tight for a full two seconds before she released em. The display of affection stunned em, and e almost missed her next words.

"I'm glad you're back to you. Don't ever do that again, especially not on my account."

Her concern wrapped snugly around em, filling em with the courage for defiance. E crossed eir arms and pushed away thoughts of all the mentors who had dismissed em before at the first sign of protest or question.

"I can't promise that," e said. "I want to help, and you're all very bad at asking for anything. I could tell it was important to you. And it turned out fine, even if it was scary! I'd do it again."

Keza huffed and poked at eir bruise as protest. "Horace, you're as good at giving as we are bad at asking, and one of these days you'll give more than you should have." The playfulness at the start of her retort vanished. She grabbed eir shoulder, her claws prickling through eir clothes just enough to command attention. "I would rather have learned nothing than to have lost you. Is that clear?"

Eir lips parted for a reply, but not a single word made it past the sudden lump in eir throat. E compensated by pulling Keza back into a hug of eir own, squeezing her tight while she leaned into em. By the time e released her, tears were streaming down eir eyes, forcing em to wipe eir cheeks. Keza patted eir shoulder.

"I did pressure Nerevin into teaching me something specifically for you. They have this game, the Birth of a Mountain? We can't play while the Wagon's moving, but I can explain it to you. And tell you how I broke it, too."

"That—that would be wonderful," e said, before plopping right back down.

Keza settled next to em and began her description with the strange hexagon in the ground at the heart of the game.

The Wagon crew spent the next two weeks crawling through the reeds and mud of the marsh. The further in they travelled, the harder the path was to follow, and the Wagon's legs sank into deep puddles and shifting ground several times a day. It cursed at the land and complained at the indignity of it all, huffing every time Keza thanked it for providing another opportunity to practise. Her newfound skills kept them moving forward even through the gruelling biome.

More than once, their inching progress was stopped entirely by another Fragment storm, forcing them all to hunker down within the Wagon. Aliyah filled the time with tales of the monastery—quiet hours tending to the vineyard, contemplative silence as dawn peeked through old windows, brutal training sessions in which Nerevin had learned to move the earth.

During the second storm, Keza joined with

uncharacteristic hesitancy. Her words halting one moment, then speeding through the tale the next, she told them of hours sparring with Nene, of the way Jael had been the only one to remain calm while Lena was giving birth, of how easily they'd settled into a rhythm, all four of them. Deep longing filled the Wagon as they listened to what she was willing to share—and when she escaped to her hammock immediately after, they all gave her the space she wanted.

Everyone's moods continued to darken as days passed in grey sameness and the marsh stretched on. The games of saira grew sullen and rarefied, Rumi hid to work on the wings prototype they'd stolen from the Archivists, and Keza put less and less heart in her morning training with Horace, obviously distracted.

Then the fog cleared at last, returning colours to the world as it vanished, and Horace discovered Rumi's map had been wrong.

The forest of Aliyah's dream was not made of twisted branches and deadly trees, as it was drawn onto it. It was lush and beautiful, the vibrant green canopy a blessing for the eyes after the endless grey of the marshes. A warbler's melodic notes greeted them, bright and cheerful, as they all gathered on top of the Wagon to admire the ocean of trunks.

They had made it.

Horace set eir hand on Aliyah's shoulder and grinned when she turned to em. "We're here," e said, as if that wasn't obvious to them all.

"Hold on tight," the Wagon declared.

It bounded forward, forcefully pulling its legs out of the mud with squelching sounds. The ground hardened as they neared the forest, the reeds ceding the way to sturdier bushes, and for a brief glorious instant the sun warmed their skin. Then they plunged under the canopy, crashing through some of the underbrush before coming to a rest. A soft breeze whispered through the leaves as the Wagon lowered itself.

"Master Rumi, I require maintenance," it said.

"Right. Got mud in your joints in addition to your brain."

Rumi vanished inside, which Horace thought

was extremely courageous after that casual mockery. The Wagon was not one to let things slide so easily—and indeed, a few seconds later they heard a cupboard slam, and Rumi's muffled protest.

"Don't give me that! You've not been able to make any sense of the wings' runes either with all the Fragments storms melting your mind." His voice cleared halfway through as he exited the Wagon from the front, a clawed hand clutched around the handle of a small toolbox, and hopped to the closest wheel, still in its leg mode. "You'll get better and then we'll figure it out."

"No mysteries can withstand me," the Wagon said, with all the grump of a comforted child.

Horace met Aliyah's gaze, and it became all but impossible to contain eir amusement once e saw it reflected there. Eir laughter bubbled out, and e leaned on top of the railing to study the thick woods before them.

"We all could use a pause before we move on," e said. Especially Keza, who'd been inordinately silent still and kept staring distractedly at the marsh. "Keza, are you feeling up for some foraging? Fresh ingredients might do wonders for our mood."

Keza startled at her name, then nodded. "Sure thing, big fella. Hopefully my nose for what's edible won't fail me now."

She leaped off the roof, landing in the brush, and within a minute e couldn't find her shape between the trees anymore. Worry instantly squeezed eir heart—should she be alone in there? Especially now? There was still so much on her mind, and they had no idea what was in the forest.

"She'll be fine," Aliyah said, reading eir fears with ease. "Some time alone and a return to routine will help her. Come on, let's see if we can aid Rumi. He might need your strength to properly clean the Wagon."

Horace knew she meant to keep em busy so e wouldn't worry so much, but e followed gratefully. Depending on what mysteries the forest held for them, it could well be their last normal night. Besides, she might be correct about Rumi.

"All right," e said, "but then I'm off to cook. I had an idea for the Inae berries—they're very sweet, and I bet they'd balance the welleran earthiness perfectly. Like Keza and Rumi!"

"That sounds delicious," Aliyah said. "Anything else in your plan?"

It was all the prompting Horace needed. As they helped clean out one of the Wagon's legs, Horace explained in great details all the meal ideas e'd been mulling over since the monastery, including some e didn't have ingredients for any longer. Time flew in a snap, and e wasn't sure e'd stopped talking at any point by the time they all sat atop the Wagon with a plate in hand.

Keza reappeared as she often did around meal hours, as if summoned by the smell. She sniffed at her plate, declared herself eager to "try this potentially sacrilegious use of the Inae berries" and plopped down next to Horace. As they ate and laughed together, the weight that had settled over em through their crossing of the marsh finally lifted.

THE STORY CONTINUES....

Fate and friendship brought the Wagon Crew together in Rumi's sentient, self-propelling wagon. Their travels across a world haunted by Fragments, dangerous shards that can possess travellers, has unravelled part of the mystery behind Aliyah's past, her strange abilities, and the Fragments themselves.

At last, they have reached the forest of Aliyah's dreams, in which they hope to find the rest of their answers. Hiding within the green foliage are the forest's magical dwelllers , small spirits with bodies of mulch, faces of bark, and eyes that shine the colour of Aliyah's magic. Their curiosity and wonder is only rivalled by Horace's, and soon the Wagon Crew is hard at work trying to communicate with them and understand their place in the puzzle.

The idyllic cultural exchange is interrupted by an assault from Archivists. They know Aliyah has reached the end of their Journey, and they intend to shape the story to their liking. The faintest hint of their presence sends the forest sprites scurrying with fear. If the Wagon Crew wants to unearth the answers they've travelled for, they will first need to confront the dangerous organization in a final stand.

A flash of green unfurled from above, snatching the last dumpling up from under Horace's fingers. Eir gaze snapped up, and e caught a blur of brown and green shuffling through the leaves, vanishing as quickly as it'd appeared.

"Hey!" e called, jumping to eir feet. "That was mine!"

E sprinted into the forest, hoping to catch another glimpse of the brown shape. Branches slapped against eir cheeks or snagged into eir clothes until e slowed down—after which e heard a chorus of chirping, tinkling sounds, like half a dozen bells swinging in a soft breeze. E crept closer to the sound's source, but a twig snapped under eir boots. Silence sliced through the tinkling chorus, sharp and tense.

"Hello?" Horace called.

An ear-splitting shriek pierced the forest, not unlike the Fragments' discordant noises, but far more melodic. Leaves shook around em as the shadows scattered, gone faster than e could truly see them, and then silence returned. Horace cast a desperate look around, as if e had better chances of spotting these creatures than e did before, and instead found the last dumpling on a small flat rock. It had been torn open, its content spilled like guts, but Horace wasn't sure any of it had actually been eaten.

E scooped up what e could with all the care in the world, as if it was a wounded baby bird and not a wasted piece of food, and examined it. All the filling was definitely still there. So why...?

A branch cracked behind em as Horace pondered, and e spun just in time to catch two shining eyes in a brown lump vanish back into the canopy again. Eir heart pounded. It had been no bigger than a fat chicken, and it definitely was watching em.

"Did you want it?" e said, placing the dumpling back down. "I could make more, no need to steal."

They took a lot of efforts, but if that's what e needed to draw the forest creatures out, e'd do it in a heartbeat.

Order the next book now at

books2read.com/tangledpast-nerezia

Join the Newsletter to get all extras and never miss an update

About the Author

Claudie Arseneault is an easily-enthused aromantic and asexual writer with a never-ending cycle of obsessions but an enduring love for all things cephalopod and fantasy (together or not!). She writes stories that centre platonic relationships and loves large casts and single-city settings, the most notable of which are the City of Spires series (2017-2023) and Baker Thief (2018).

In addition to her own fiction, Claudie has co-edited Common Bonds (2021), an anthology of aromantic speculative short stories. She is a founding member of The Kraken Collective, an alliance of self-publishing SFF authors, and the creator of the Aromantic and Asexual Characters Database.

Find out more at claudiearseneault.com

Start another book from the Kraken Collective!

Craving more fun bite-sized queer fantasy? Party of Fools is a comedic adventure with big Final Fantasy vibes where two rebels tag along as the Chosen One and imperial Hero escapes scrutiny to go on a worldwide food tour—that is, if she can escape the Capital.

Dig into another novella lead by a non-binary protagonist and thaes close-knit group of friends with *The Shimmering Prayer of Sûkiurâq*, A deliciously queer magical person story in a secondary world with floating cities and airships, perfect for fans of She-Ra and Steven Universe.

Find these books and more at
www.krakencollectivebooks.com

Acknowledgements

Another year begins, and with it comes another Nerezia adventure. What a blast I had drafting this one, too! Thank you for coming along "Keza's episode," an homage to training montages and elemental magic in fantasy.

Every time I come to the acknowledgements, I wish I had something deep to say. But the truth is ever the same: I would not be here without readers picking up my books, friends and family supporting me, fellow authors sharing writing woes and wins.

A specific thank you to my production team: Eva with the eternally gorgeous covers, Lynn with the editing, as well as every writer with whom I've sprinted. I always appreciate the company, but *Lost Traditions* especially needed me to have others grounding me.

And now… only two novellas left to conclude a big storyarc. Onward!

9 781069 251671